The Proposal

"I KNOW I'm twice your age, Rose. But a lot of marriages are like that. I know in many ways you are still a child, yet in so many others you are an enchanting young lady. If you marry me, I promise to honor both those qualities in you."

I didn't want to look into his blue eyes. For I knew I would be lost if I did.

"I know you don't love me. I don't expect you to in the beginning. I hope to earn that love. I know I must."

I said nothing.

"But I love you. You should know that. I want to give you time, of course. I know you need more time."

He had thrown me a lifeline! "Yes, please, give me some time to think on it. It's all so new to me."

He had taken my hand and now he released it and tucked my hair on the left side behind my ear. "I fell in love with you the first time I saw you, Rose."

Brooklyn Rose

OTHER NOVELS BY ANN RINALDI

Or Give Me Death
A Novel of Patrick Henry's Family

The Staircase

The Coffin Quilt
The Feud between the Hatfields and the McCoys

Cast Two Shadows
The American Revolution in the South

An Acquaintance with Darkness

Hang a Thousand Trees with Ribbons
The Story of Phillis Wheatley

Keep Smiling Through

The Secret of Sarah Revere

Finishing Becca
A Story about Peggy Shippen and Benedict Arnold

The Fifth of March
A Story of the Boston Massacre

A Break with Charity
A Story about the Salem Witch Trials

A Ride into Morning
The Story of Tempe Wick

ANN RINALDI

Brooklyn Rose

HARCOURT, INC.

Orlando Austin New York San Diego Toronto London

www.HarcourtBooks.com

First Harcourt paperback edition 2006

The Library of Congress has cataloged the
hardcover edition as follows:
Rinaldi, Ann.
Brooklyn Rose/Ann Rinaldi.
p.   cm.
Summary: On St. Helena Island, South Carolina,
fifteen-year-old Rose meets and marries Rene, a Yankee from
Brooklyn, New York, who takes her north to his home, where
she encounters many differences in attitudes and lifestyles.
[1. Coming of age—Fiction.   2. Marriage—Fiction.
3. Love—Fiction.]   I. Title.
PZ7.R459Bt   2005
[Fic]—dc22   2004002372
ISBN-13: 978-0-15-205117-4   ISBN-10: 0-15-205117-1
ISBN-13: 978-0-15-205538-7 pb   ISBN-10: 0-15-205538-x pb

Text set in Stempel Garamond
Designed by Cathy Riggs

A C E G H F D B

Printed in the United States of America

In memory of my grandparents
Rose and Rene

Brooklyn Rose

PART ONE

Beaufort County, South Carolina

1899–1900

1

December 16, 1899

MY BIRTHDAY. Why does one feel so special on her birthday, as if something is about to happen? I received many lovely presents, including this gilt-edged journal book from Daddy. The pages are creamy white and just waiting for my words. They even smell nice, as if they are scented. I'm so excited about it.

More excited than I am over the new Gibson Girl shirtwaist Mama gave me or the hair ribbons from my sister.

I'm writing in my new journal this very moment. What shall I say? What could possibly be good enough about my silly old dull life to put down in here?

It is a cold, drizzly day with rain. Some workers are ginning cotton and others are killing the last of the beef. Daddy sold a pair of turkeys to old Mrs. Lewis for a dollar and fifty cents. Oh, this is all so ordinary! But Mama says everything is worth setting down, that someday my granddaughter may read this. Ho! Me with a granddaughter! Imagine!

Here is something worth noting. The Gullah people who live and work around here believe that when you die your soul goes to God but your spirit stays on earth and takes part in all the activities of your people. I like that part of their belief. If I died of a sudden, I'd like my spirit to stay here.

Well, I'm not dying, at least I don't plan to yet, but Daddy talks constantly these days about sending me to school in the North, where I would get a proper American education.

Imagine that! Yankee land. And his own uncle Sumner killed at Chancellorsville!

"North is the only place you have chances," Daddy says. "The chances are all done around here."

Chances for what? I want to ask. But I know he'd say, "To marry the right person." He wants me to wed somebody with money. "Even though that person is a Yankee?" I'd ask. To which he'd say, "The only ones who have money are the Yankees."

This family has had such a problem with money since the war ended thirty-five years ago.

I know one thing. I'm not ever going north. I'm staying right here on Saint Helena's Island. Why, Daddy was only able to buy the house back the year I was born. I know he spent most of his money restoring it to what it was before the war and hasn't got much to dower me with. But I've only just turned fifteen, and he's doing well with the cotton and the horses. We have the best horse farm in the county. And how could I leave here, anyway?

I know another thing, too. If I ever do go away, I'm going to leave my spirit here to help my family. Like the Gullah people do when they die.

MAYBE I OUGHT to get things down right, if I'm going to keep this as a proper journal. The house I sit in, the very room I sit in, is on Saint Helena's Island, off the coast of South Carolina. I'm so used to this place I think everyone should know of it. Certainly they should, upon second thought. Wouldn't it be wonderful if everyone lived in a house made of a strong tabby foundation with a double piazza held up by great pillars and a front yard that sloped down to the water? If everyone could hear the wind in the palmetto trees and taste the sand in their mouths when the wind blew? And what about the tides that flow toward land twice each day, then back out again?

To say nothing of the wild ducks and the swampy lands and the cypress trees, the longleaf pine. And the sea oats on the sand dunes that keep the sand from being washed away.

This house I sit in was built years ago by my great-grandfather. My grandparents lost it when General Sherman came through and burned a lot of the homes around here. The white owners were driven away. But General Sherman left this house and a few others standing so the Negroes could live in them and work the land. Then Yankee agents went from plantation to plantation and took the cotton and shipped it north.

My Grandfather Frampton had to go to work as a teacher in the Freedman's School here on the island because he was so destitute after the war. I recollect Grandmother Frampton telling us, before she died, how he looked of a morning when he would get ready to go to work, this wonderful gentleman who'd once been rich and owned dozens of slaves. How she'd hear him early in the morning in the kitchen, getting his own lunch pail ready and moving about quietly. How she couldn't get up to help him for fear of embarrassing him. And how he'd go off, day after day, like a common workingman to earn his living. They were living in a log cabin on the island then, even though this house was still standing. He made sixty dollars a month. Grandmother Frampton couldn't abide seeing him so demeaned, so she started making pies. Not sweet potato and pecan like they do hereabouts, but fruit and cream like they do up north, since that was where she came from. And soon they had to hire people to help her because the pies sold so fast. She made a fortune, so Grandfather didn't have to teach anymore. And that fortune they left to Daddy, who was able to buy this place back for the family. I'm so proud of him for doing that.

Now my daddy grows his cotton again. And breeds his horses. Right now we have thirteen mares and two stallions, and five two-year-olds to be broken to the saddle and bridle before they get shipped to Lexington for the horse auctions.

The pie business is sold. And we're well-off. But still Daddy wants me to go north to school. We have relatives in Connecticut, from Grandmother's connections.

Oh, sometimes the future frightens me so

much, I don't want to grow up. I want to be a young girl forever. But I do have opinions. We were brought up in this family to have opinions, but Mama says a proper young lady shouldn't voice hers too loudly or her husband will think her forward and brash. And so I am forward and brash. My husband will just have to abide that in me.

2

December 17

I HAVE A LITTLE brother named Benjamin, who is fourteen months old and the most cunning baby I have ever known. He toddles about now, getting into everything. I'm jealous of Lilly, who is our Opal's daughter, because she is assigned by Mama to watch him. Mama says I have better things to do, like studying or working on my sewing. Opal and Lilly and all the other help we have here are descended from the Gullah slaves who used to work for my grandparents. Of course, they aren't slaves anymore. Daddy pays them right well. Still, they could leave anytime but don't. They have a loyalty to my family.

The Gullah people believe the strangest things. They believe that to stop a hooty owl from hooting, you should cross your fingers, take off a shoe, and turn it over. Because a hooting owl is a bad omen. Then you have to point your finger in the direction of the sound, put a poker in the fire, and squeeze your right wrist with your left hand. Never mind that by the time you get to the wrist-squeezing part, the owl has flown away.

I'm the middle child. My older sister, Heppi, is seventeen going on twenty-five, and everything I do, according to her lights, is wrong. Sometimes she is so snobbish and picks on me so much that I hate her outright. When she plagues me, I threaten to tell people what her real name is. It's Hephzibah. Isn't that terrible? She is named after Grandmother Frampton, who made the pies. Heppi's middle name is Maria, and that's what she wants us to call her, but nobody does. I'm so glad I wasn't born first, or I'd have that name. My name is Rose.

Heppi has beaux all over the place. The way she flirts is shameful. I couldn't do that if I tried. But, somehow, when I see how the boys respond to her, I envy her so much I could die.

I don't like many of her beaux, but one I think is very nice. His name is Joshua Denning, and he is down here from the North to collect Negro music and publish it in a book. He goes about Beaufort, on the mainland, and this and other islands, listening to the Negroes sing. He goes into their churches and their homes. I think it is so decent of him to honor their work like that. I also think he is too good for Heppi.

I love holding Benjamin. He used to fit just right into the crook of my arm, but he is too big for that now. I love his dimpled face, his little fists, his fat arms. And when he smiles at me with those eyes of his and that crooked little smile, I just melt into nothing. Oh, I think it would be so good sometimes to be married and to have him be mine.

I am making him a new embroidered nightgown of white lawn in my spare moments.

I'm writing this early in the morning. I must go down to breakfast.

DADDY WAS out hunting when I took breakfast. He killed four ducks and came back for the noon meal. Eight of "his people," as he calls the help, are down with the ague. Little Benjamin was cranky and I took him in the sunporch, where the sun was lovely coming in the windows and the stove was lit. I put him to sleep for Mama, because Lilly is one who has the ague. Mama sent for the doctor for the Negroes who are ill even though they have their own remedies, like cockroach tea for coughing.

Opal has the ague, too. And she's our cook. She runs the kitchen and sometimes the whole house. I made one of Grandmother's pies. Mama can still cook, but Opal sent her other daughter, Ruth, in to take her place. We made an excellent supper, if I must say so myself. Fresh wild duck that Daddy brought home from his hunting expedition.

Joshua Denning was at the noon meal with us. I'd forgotten that Heppi was supposed to accompany him today on one of his calls to do an interview about Negro music. Heppi took advantage of his presence to ask me for my good blue velvet cloak to wear. I didn't want to give it. "You have yours, trimmed with ermine," I said, to which she replied, "It's cloth, not velvet."

Well, what does she want to show off in front of the Negroes for, anyway? But she must have it, of course, just like she must have everything she wants. Mama indulges her so. Mama always takes up for her because she's the oldest. I was near tears when Mama said how lovely Heppi looked in my cloak. Mr. Denning did nothing but smoke his pipe and smile at her. I declare, he is smitten. And what means does he have? Why, plenty, or you can be assured Daddy would never let him be courting my sister. His father is a captain of industry, Mama says. They are from Pennsylvania and his father does something important with coal up there. I do like Josh, and if he weren't so smitten I'd like him for myself. Is that terrible to say?

I'm fifteen now and Mama and Daddy

have been looking at me and thinking of my marriage. I just know it. Time to grow up. I'm a woman.

Then why do I still get ordered around? It pleases my family to treat me like a woman, it seems, when they want me to act like one. But otherwise I'm still considered a child.

December 18

TODAY DADDY had an accident with the carriage. He had taken Mama and little Benjamin for a ride, since the day was fine. Becky Sharp and Little Dorrit were pulling the carriage. I should say here that Daddy names all his horses after characters in stories from England. Jimmy, Opal's son, was holding the reins.

They were crossing the bridge on the causeway over the sands when a plank in the bridge gave way, and the two horses fell through the opening that was caused when more planks broke. They both fell in backward and clung with their front legs to the remaining bridge while Daddy got Mama and little Benjamin out. Jimmy was holding the reins in front of the horses so they wouldn't fall through, and somehow together they managed to hoist Becky Sharp and Little Dorrit out of the opening. The horses were cut and bruised, and Daddy was very upset. But the horses brought them home. Daddy had Jimmy bathe the horses and rub them down with ointment, and they are resting.

To think what could have happened! Mama and little Benjamin in such danger. Oh, my heart stops and my hands shake thinking of it. I never dwell on death, but Daddy always says it is around us all the time. I am beginning to believe him.

AS IF ALL THAT weren't enough, later on in the day Daddy had to go to my great-grandmother and -grandfather's grave because it is the anniversary of their death in 1860. What it is, really, is a vault. And during the war Yankees broke it open to look for treasure. These days it is somewhat in disrepair, and Daddy always means to get it fixed. I don't know why people had to have vaults. No wonder the Yankees thought it contained treasure. It is very large and carved with lots of angels.

TODAY IN school I got into a disagreement with Amelia Caper. She is one of those people who is your friend one moment and saying something mean to you the next, so that you are so confused you don't know what she is. But you must pay mind to her, because if you don't you might miss something.

She has her nose up in the air so much I'm surprised birds haven't poked twigs in it. She said my daddy owes her daddy money from way back to Grandmother Frampton's time, that her daddy, who owns the bank, loaned Grandmother money to start her pie business and we never paid it back. Amelia's daddy knows everybody's business because he is a banker. And she must listen at home because she seems to know it all, too. And she holds it over everybody in school.

When I came home, I asked Daddy and he said it wasn't true. Amelia thinks she is so special because her father drives one of those new-type automobiles. I think it is ugly. And I'll wager if it fell through the planks on the bridge, it would never be able to take them home again, like Becky Sharp and Little Dorrit did.

I go to the village school. This is my last year. Mama says next year if I don't go north, I must go to Normal School in Beaufort, which means I will board there. I don't want to go away from home.

3

December 23

I HAVE HAD a dreadful cold so I have not
written in this book for days. The wind has
been blowing sand all over the place outside,
and inside the fires are warm and comforting.
I especially like it around the big black stove in
the kitchen. Opal always has something good
cooking there. I wander around the house,

taking some pills the doctor left, and then taking some remedies from Opal and her people. I figure between both worlds I should get better. Still, I look terrible and I feel terrible, and I would like to curl up and hibernate like a bear. My hair needs washing and Mama won't let me wash it until my cold is gone, and that makes me feel even worse.

We are all getting ready for Christmas. I'm helping Heppi, bad as I feel, and Daddy has promised us a tree for the front parlor.

Heppi is going to sing in the choir in church and has been practicing. She fancies herself a regular opera singer. If I never hear another Christmas song I will be the happiest person on earth.

Before my cold got bad, Daddy took us in the boat to Beaufort to shop for Christmas presents. Since it's a very long trip and we needed the afternoon to shop, we stayed over at the very elegant Sea Island Hotel, and

Daddy had supper with his "girls" in the dining room. What a lark! I bought a journal for Heppi. I think she should be keeping one, as I do. I have saved my money for my presents all on my own, money I got from doing chores around the place. And then Mama surprised me by giving me five whole dollars for all the times I took care of Benjamin for her, when Lilly wasn't able. I felt so rich!

I bought Daddy two books on the history of Beaufort County, and Mama a fringed shawl. I bought Benjamin a play-pretty that spins on the floor when you wind a string around it and let it loose. I can't wait for him to see it.

December 24

CHRISTMAS EVE. We all went to church and it was so very cold. I was hoping Daddy would say it was too cold, but we went to hear Heppi sing in the choir. Afterward I saw Josh Denning kissing her in the cloakroom. I think they will become betrothed soon. Heppi's eyes glow these days like Christmas candles. I wonder what it is like to be in love. I wonder if my eyes will ever glow like that. I wonder if a man will ever love me, just because I am me. Can you imagine that?

Mama says Heppi is lucky because she and Daddy approve of Josh, and Heppi loves him. She says most girls our age have arranged marriages, and many times love does not come into it.

December 25

CHRISTMAS DAY. Opal came to my room early, carrying a torch of light wood because it was still dark. She lit the fire in the fireplace then came to lean over me, as she did every morning. "Room be warm," she said. "Little girl get up."

I waited a few minutes so the underclothes she laid over the screen in front of the fire would be warm. Then I jumped up and dressed. Oh, warm underclothes are so delicious!

Downstairs, Mama made us drink hot chocolate and have a biscuit before we opened presents. Daddy lit the candles on the tree, and we all opened gifts. Soon we had to put the candles out because Benjamin wanted to grab them. I got a new saddle and saddle blanket from Daddy and Mama and three books. Little Benjamin got lots of play-pretties. My family loved the gifts I gave them.

Then we all went into the dining room for a hearty Christmas breakfast. Daddy looked at the outside thermometer and said he never remembered it being so cold. At noontime, in the sun, the thermometer read ten degrees. Icicles are hanging from all the outside buildings in back of the house. I took an apple to my horse, Tom Jones, and I put a special blanket over his back. After Christmas dinner I rode him around the plantation, and steam came out of his nostrils.

We had delicious pound cake and oranges, and I was even allowed a sip of champagne at supper. I felt very grown-up. The cake is the same recipe that Mama and Daddy had for their wedding cake. Mama made it special, and I am going to make it one of these days. Josh Denning came and was in the back parlor with Daddy a long time. I think he was asking for Heppi's hand. He brought presents for all of us, and I wished I had one for him. He gave me a spyglass I have always yearned for. I think he is a lovely catch for Heppi.

December 31

THE LAST DAY of 1899. Daddy and Mama had some friends in, and there was much gaiety and gossip. I was allowed to stay up until after midnight and I should be in bed now, but I just had to write down what happened. Mr. Scully, the newspaper editor, told us that he received word today that Sioux Indian chief Spotted Tail died in Paris. He was one of the most famous war chiefs of the Sioux tribe.

Everyone was wondering what the new century will bring. It's very scary. The turn of the century. Mr. and Mrs. Caper came but not Amelia. She had another party. Mr. Caper didn't look at all as if Daddy owed him money.

The Capers brought with them a gentleman friend everyone whispered about, who is very handsome and is supposedly French. He is tall. I'll wager over six feet. And he has broad shoulders and a slim waist. He bears himself with grace. His hair is a mixed brown and blond, as is his mustache, and he has a presence about him. He spoke very precise English, and when Daddy was talking to him, he called me over to introduce me.

I crossed the room, even though I was shaking inside. Just looking at the man made me shaky and excited.

"This is Mr. Dumarest," Daddy said. "He has business in Charleston."

I remembered to curtsy as I've been taught. Daddy seemed very proud of me and anxious to show me off. Mr. Dumarest asked me about our horses. His eyes are so blue you could drown in them. His face is strong. There is nothing about him that isn't sure and strong. His voice is masterful.

The announcement was made tonight. Heppi and Josh will wed on Valentine's Day. Heppi was flustered when Daddy announced it. She even managed to look like a bashful bride. From across the room, I saw Mr. Dumarest watching me, and I felt very uncomfortable.

Later on, when we were getting ready for bed, Heppi came into my room and asked me to be her maid of honor. I couldn't believe it!

Then she hugged me and we sat a long time talking on my bed. She told me how she loved Joshua, how his book of Negro music would soon be published and he was going to dedicate it to her. And how they were going to live in a fine house in Beaufort. She said they were looking at the James Rhett house at 303 Federal Street.

For the first time, I felt like we were sisters. Then she told me how Mr. Dumarest had offered Daddy some silk for her wedding dress. "He imports silk," she said. "He's offered silk for your dress, too."

I blushed that he had thought of me and what dress I should wear.

"He's been doing business with Mr. Caper forever. And Daddy has known him for quite a while," Heppi told me.

Then she leaned forward and said quietly, "Rose, it's time you knew. Daddy isn't doing so well financially. I've known it for some while. Don't tell him I told you, but he has debts he can't meet."

The way she said it frightened me. "What has this to do with the silk?" I asked her.

"You've got to marry soon, Rose. When Daddy has two daughters who are well married, things will be easier for him."

"Is that why he showed me off to Mr. Dumarest tonight?" I asked.

She smiled. "Don't tell me you weren't attracted to him."

"That has nothing to do with it. I felt like a horse at an auction."

"You could do worse." And she giggled.

I blushed and thought of his blue eyes, his regal bearing, his confidence. "Don't be silly," I said. "Now go to sleep."

4

January 1, 1900

IT SEEMS SO strange to write "1900." I can't get used to it. A whole new century stretching out in front of us. What will happen? Heppi says it doesn't make any difference, that neither God nor the universe knows it is another century, that only we humans make a fuss over time. But she was having one of her sophisticated moments.

Amelia's father has a telephone in his house, but we don't have one yet. He is talking about getting a steam generator to have his own electricity in his home. When that happens, Amelia won't be bearable.

Mr. Dumarest was back today for New Year's dinner. He seems so comfortable at our table, but I was self-conscious, thinking of what Heppi told me. Are Mama and Daddy planning on wedding me to him? Why, he must be in his thirties, at least. And, oh, I couldn't be married. The very thought of it frightens me.

But I am attracted to him. And I find myself watching him when he doesn't know it. I like to watch the way he moves and holds his head. And when he looks at me, I want to dive under the table.

Still, everything seemed normal until Daddy

asked me, after dinner, to take Mr. Dumarest out to the stables to see the horses. It seems he wants to purchase one.

So I put on my coat, trembling. Mr. Dumarest helped me with it. He opened doors. He kept the conversation going. He was so gallant. I felt like a clod, like I was blushing all over.

We ventured out back to the barn. I showed him the paddock where Jimmy and Daddy break the horses. In the barn, Jimmy was there to welcome us.

He showed Mr. Dumarest the new cotton gin Daddy had bought and the other farm machinery. I showed him all the horses in their stalls. Then I showed him the small office Daddy had off the barn, and the leather books that had all the breeding records. He liked everything, especially the old buggy that used to belong to Grandmother and Grandfather Frampton. "This is the one they left in when you Yankees and General Sherman put them out," I told him.

Well, that's enough to get anybody talking. His eyes shone with amusement. "I wasn't born yet when that happened," he said. "And, anyway, when I was born it was in France."

We patted the horses. I noticed he has a way with them. He turned and looked at me. "We ought to go riding someday while I'm here," he said to me.

I blushed. I could not look into those eyes, because I felt that they saw all of me, all my secret hopes and fears. "Yes, someday we should ride together," I said, which sounded too forward, so then I went mum. Thank heaven for Jimmy's man chatter with him.

On the way back to the house, we talked more. "I'd love to see the whole place sometime," Mr. Dumarest said. "Perhaps you can take me about when we ride." He spoke with a slight French accent.

"When did you come to this country?" I asked.

He smiled. "About five years ago. I came with my brother, Adrian. We're in business together."

"Is Adrian older?"

More smile. "Yes."

"Does he boss you about?"

"No. We're business partners. We import silk. We have two warehouses, one here and one in New York."

I gasped. "Oh, tell me about New York! I've always wanted to go there." And then I blushed some more.

"In five minutes?" he asked.

"No, of course not," I said demurely. "Some other time, maybe."

"Yes. When you take me on that ride about the place. Oh, what color silk do you like? I'm to bring some for you and your sister next time I come."

"It isn't my choice," I told him. "It's up to Heppi. It's her wedding. Mama says she gets to run the whole thing." But then I told him, "During the War of Secession, my grandmother made a flag of blue silk with a palmetto tree on it for the Saint Helena's Volunteers. We still have it up in the attic. I think it is so pretty."

"Then I'll ask Heppi if I may bring you blue. In memory of your grandmother," he said.

Why is it that when we went back into the house I felt as if I had the edge on everyone else, as if I knew him better than anyone in the family? Why did I feel just a little taller? When he left he asked my father if he could come around this week and ride with me. That he had a horse all picked out. My daddy said yes.

"You have a date," Heppi whispered as we went upstairs to bed.

"Don't be silly," I said. "He's way too old

for me. He's got to be thirty, at least. I'm just helping Daddy sell a horse."

January 4

MR. DUMAREST purchased from Daddy a light sorrel mare with a star on her forehead. Since she was not named as yet, he asked me to help him think of a name for her. But first he took her out riding.

I thought that Mama would insist we take Heppi along for a chaperone, but she did no such thing. And Daddy did not insist, either. He knows me too well. He knows I would never suffer mistreatment from a man. And he knows Rene, too, I suppose.

Rene said I was to call him that. By his first name. "If we're going to be friends, I insist," he told me.

Daddy had half his people picking cotton and the other half gathering wood. Rene had never seen cotton being picked, so I took him by those fields first, then we rode to the water. The day was a bit warmer, with bright sun. I explained to him how when the moon is in its first and third quarters, the tides rise six to eight feet around Saint Helena's Island. These are called neap tides.

"When the moon is new or full, the water rises eight to ten feet. And those are spring tides," I explained.

He listened carefully, nodding.

"Saint Helena's is fifteen miles long and three to five miles wide. It protects the mainland from the sea."

"You've learned your school lessons well," he said.

"Those aren't school lessons. School is dull," I told him. "I've learned these other things just from living around here."

He asked me if I liked living here, and I said yes. Then he asked if I would ever leave.

The way he said it, with those blue eyes of his looking so intently at me, I couldn't answer. "I don't know," I finally said. "It would depend."

"On what?"

"On why I was leaving." I felt bold saying it. He did not reply.

Then we rode on farther. I took him through salt marshes, up dunes. I showed him massive oak trees, twisted cedars and crooked pines, and palmettos with leaves that rattled in the wind like the drums of the Yamasee Indians.

We got back in time for afternoon tea. I was red faced from the wind. Rene's tawny hair was mussed. He told Daddy he'd like to go fishing with him sometime. And Daddy said yes.

January 8

BACK TO school after the winter break. Amelia Caper was waiting for me with a wide smile on her face. "Your daddy told mine that you went riding with Mr. Dumarest," she said.

"Rene and I are just friends," I said.

But when I called him Rene instead of Mr. Dumarest, her grin got sly. "He's looking for a wife, you know," she said smugly.

"Well then," I told her, "you ought to get in line. I understand half the girls between here and Charleston are lying in wait for him."

"And you've got him."

"I've got nobody, Amelia. I don't want anybody. Why, he's older than Josh Denning, and he's twenty-four."

I wouldn't hear any more about it. Amelia thinks she is so smart because of her daddy the banker. I hate being back in school. Before he was eight years old, Daddy was sent to school 150 miles from home. To Richland. Sometimes, when people annoy me, I wish I could go 150 miles from here and from everyone. Other times I don't want to leave home at all.

Daddy went to the trial of skill with his rifle company today so was not home for supper. It's been very windy all day. Wind has whipped the sand in all our faces. Mama and Heppi and I had supper alone and discussed the wedding. All Heppi wants to do is talk about the wedding. She says blue silk is all right for my dress, and Mama said she'd send a note around to Mr. Dumarest. I have not told them yet that I call him Rene.

5

January 10

I HAVE BEEN getting teased in school about
Rene. It seems Amelia Caper has told everyone
about him taking me riding. My daddy told her
daddy. I am so sick of this school and have
asked Daddy if I can go to Normal School in
Beaufort. Or the Female Institute. He always
said he wanted me to go to one of them to get a

better education before I go to any female institute up north. But when we talk about it, he
never pursues the subject. He lets it lie like a
dead fish between us. I think it is likely that he
does not have the money. I am beginning to
wonder if he is more in debt than he allows.

January 14

RENE HAS sent around the silk for Heppi's
wedding gown and it is absolutely gorgeous.
Mama cried when she saw it. So is the blue for
my dress. And I fear it is of a more expensive
quality than Daddy can afford, but he said
nothing.

On the weekend, Mama and Heppi and I
had meetings with the dressmaker in Beaufort.
We stayed at the hotel. I know Mama was half
distracted wondering after little Benjamin, but
Lilly and Opal do a wonderful job with him. I
missed him, too.

On Saturday evening Rene came to town and took the three of us to supper. He told us all about the silk-importing business. He owns a fifteen-ton schooner called *Elizabeth*. He paid mind mostly to Mama, because she was really the prettiest of us there. My mama is really beautiful. We have a portrait of her in the front hallway and she is painted in profile. Her hair is piled on top of her head and her shoulders are bare and the gown puffs around them.

Still, Heppi flirted with him like mad. It is just her way. She made me so angry I wanted to cry. She placed herself right across the table from him so he could look directly at her and monopolized all the conversation. But several times I saw Rene sneaking looks at me. And I blushed. I wonder: Why is he paying all this attention to us? Heppi is spoken for and Mama is nobody's flirt.

We came home this evening. Rene is invited to the wedding, of course.

January 16

A VERY NICE day with almost springlike
weather. Daddy's people planted Irish potatoes today, and finished ginning the cotton.
Little Benjamin is very cranky. I just discov-
ered that we are invited to go with Heppi and
Josh to the Eckelses' on Saturday night for
a program of sacred music. Rene is calling to
take Mama and me. Daddy has a dinner at his
club. I don't know if I am pleased or not. It
seems that all kinds of things are being done
to throw me and Rene together, and I wonder,
sometimes, just what Amelia Caper knows.
Somehow I feel that she knows something.

January 21

WELL, WE WENT to the Eckelses' and Rene
couldn't have been nicer. He fussed over Mama
just as much as he fussed over me. I am starting to look at him differently, though. I am

asking myself very stern questions, like, "Is he acting like a suitor?" and, "What am I supposed to act like?" and, "I must put a stop to this. But how can I?" I wouldn't want to hurt him, and somehow I think I'd be hurting Mama and Daddy, too, because by now I know they want him for me.

Next week Rene is going hunting on one of the other islands with Daddy. Josh was pleased with the Negro music at the Eckelses'. Daddy sent a load of cotton to Beaufort for sale. The boat was piled high with cotton.

Two of the two-year-olds have been broken to the saddle and bridle by Jimmy. I watched. He is so good with the horses. I told Daddy he has to have Jimmy teach somebody else, though, in case he ever decides to leave. Daddy just laughed. "My people never leave," he said. "I treat them too good."

Of course, I know it is unthinkable, but I

have watched Jimmy in the paddock with the horses so much that I know I could break a two-year-old if push came to shove. Only, I would never say it to either Daddy or Mama. They think I'm enough of a hoyden the way it is.

February 5

MAMA IS ALL upset because a steamer arrived in San Francisco and there are forty-one deaths from the plague on it. These things upset Mama terribly. She worries so. I suppose the city officials in San Francisco were upset, too, because to stop the spread of the disease they burned down a whole block in Chinatown and the fire got out of control.

Went to Beaufort with Mama for a final fitting of our gowns. I declare, Heppi is acting like a five-year-old now, who has just been given candy. All she talks about is her wedding. She wanted to have it in church, but Daddy and Mama want it in our front parlor. Mama says she always dreamed of her daughter marrying in that room, because it faces the rising sun and that is good luck.

Well, much discussion about this. Church or home? Home, of course. What other way? Mama says. This is tradition. So now Mama is directing the help (or Opal is letting her think she is directing) in cleaning and polishing and shining and washing everything in sight. The house is turned upside down. I hate it.

February 7

DADDY AND RENE never did take their hunting trip. Everything seemed to interfere. The *Elizabeth* dropped anchor in Charleston waters with a new load of silk and Rene couldn't get away. One of Daddy's workhorses came down with distemper and had to be nursed. So they are going when they both have time. Probably not until after Heppi's wedding now. I wish I could go, not to be with Rene but because I've never been on a hunting trip with Daddy.

Why do I have the feeling that something is about to happen?

February 10

THE HOUSE is all in order and the cooking and baking have begun. Opal has an army of people under her in the kitchen, including Mama and me. Heppi is nowhere to be seen. She is up in her room, dreaming of the great day. I chopped nuts all morning for one of Opal's cakes. Heppi dreamed of a gray horse last night, and Opal says that means an upcoming happy marriage.

February 11

THERE IS NO time to think of anything but the wedding. Josh's family arrived in Charleston and we all met in Beaufort. Daddy arranged it. We had supper at the hotel in their famous dining room. Josh's parents are nice, and he has a sister my age named Alice. They are all very proud of Josh. His father looks like a captain of industry, which he is. He owns many coal mines. Josh refused to go into the business and went into studying music instead. His brother, Jeff, is in business with their father. Rene was not there. The hotel had an orchestra and I danced with Jeff. He asked me about the Gullah people, and I explained to him how we are still under Reconstruction here in Beaufort. "We're different from the rest of the South," I told him. "Reconstruction here is still going on because most of the people who lived here before the war are gone. And the blacks own a lot of the land. And we have a lot of newcomers. There are a few old planters, like my father."

With the next dance he told me about the Amish in Pennsylvania, and I was fascinated. And a feeling came over me that there are so many different kinds of people in this world whom I shall never know. And they are interesting and good and I will never get to meet them. And I felt small and useless.

We came home this night and didn't stay at the hotel.

6

February 13

OPAL THINKS it awful of us that we are not having Heppi's wedding in church. She calls it a "praise house." She told me how her people were converted to Christianity after the war, by missionaries, although they kind of mix Gullah traditions and songs in with it.

She says she has the praise-making spirit. I explained to her how, while we are good Episcopalians now, our ancestors were Huguenots who came here in 1685 when Huguenots came from all parts of France, and we came because we were persecuted. And that's why we are free of spirit.

We had a rehearsal for the wedding and a grand supper. Heppi put up my hair so I will have proper curls tomorrow. While she was doing it, I asked her how it felt to be going away with a man on a wedding trip.

"I trust Josh and I love him and that's all that is needed," she said. "And it will serve you right to remember that when your time comes."

February 14

WELL, HEPPI GOT married. She is now Mrs. Denning. Oh, the wedding was so beautiful.

Heppi and I had made an arch of paper flowers, red and white, under which she and Josh stood. She looked so lovely in her gown. I cried when she said the words. To think that you say a few words and your life is changed forever!

We ate a sumptuous wedding supper. Opal really outdid herself, bringing dish after dish to the table. And Mama made the same wedding cake that she and Daddy had had. Later we danced in the front parlor, which had been cleared of furniture. I danced with Rene, and he said I looked wonderful in my blue silk dress. Somehow I felt that I did when he said it.

Heppi and Josh are on their wedding trip to Savannah. I can't believe it. My sister isn't my sister anymore. She belongs to someone else now. Opal sprinkled dust at her when they left, for good luck. I hope it wasn't goofer dust, because that comes from the graveyard.

February 15

SOMETHING has happened. Something changed. I felt it when I came in from riding this morning. The slant of light itself was changed inside the house.

Then Mama told me that Rene was in the library with Daddy last night after the wedding. The door was closed a long time after Heppi and Josh left. I had gone to bed and thought nothing of it until today.

At lunch today, with one daughter scarce gone and still surrounded by the Chinese lanterns strung for the wedding, and all the other furbelows, Daddy told me that Rene has asked for my hand in marriage.

I could not speak. My jaw fell open. And yet I know, deep down, I had been expecting this. I knew something was about to happen. Still, it came as a shock.

Daddy smiled. "I think the spirit of the wedding seized him," he said.

Opal was standing over me, about to pour my coffee. "He be a good man," she said. "I have many a talk with that young man." Which was true. Rene had made friends of her. She had served him many a cup of coffee when they were alone in the kitchen.

"But I'm only fifteen," was the first thing that came to my mind.

"Your mother was fifteen when we wed," Daddy said.

Mama looked so happy, still beaming from the spirit of the wedding, that I hated to ruin it for her. "Mama?" I said.

She smiled at me. "Follow your heart, Rose," she told me. "Just don't let fear into it. There's nothing to be afraid of."

"But where would we live?"

And there was the trick. They both said Brooklyn. I asked, "Where is this Brooklyn?"

And they told me it is in New York. So far away! Why, it would mean leaving here, leaving Mama and Daddy and little Benjamin. He'd grow up without me.

Then Mama said, "You like Rene, don't you, Rose? I've seen how you look at him."

"Yes," I answered lamely, "but not as a husband. I mean, I'm not in love with him."

"That will come later," Mama answered, "like it did with your father and me. He was sixteen years older than me. And we made a good marriage."

I could not believe we were discussing this so calmly. But we were.

I felt a roaring in my ears. I didn't love Rene. Did he love me? I know girls marry for reasons other than love. But I always said I wouldn't do that.

"I think I want to go back to my riding," I said. And that's exactly what I did. I went to the stable, to where there were animals and people and things that I know and can trust. I had Jimmy saddle Tom Jones again, and we went out to the sand dunes, riding. Then I took him down to the water's edge and talked to him. "Brooklyn," I told him. "Can you imagine? I've heard of Brooklyn. They have a place called Coney Island that is absolutely exciting! But I won't go. And you know what, Tom? If I have to go, I'm taking you with me. I won't leave you. Not ever."

Back at the house, I lay on my bed and I cried. Because somehow I had the feeling that time had ahold of me by the back of my neck, like our cats hold their kittens, and was shaking me and wouldn't let me go.

I thought of Rene, of the nice things about him. He was refined. A real gentleman. He'd always been gentle and respectful to me. And I thought of his blue eyes.

That afternoon the buggy from the local florist came by with a bouquet of roses. I looked out the window and saw the man carry them in. Too late for the wedding, I thought. And then Mama called up the stairs. "Rose, Rose, come down. Someone just delivered flowers for you."

They were from Rene. The card read, "From an admirer, Rene."

He is coming tonight, and I sit here writing. Oh, what time is it? I must fix my hair and get dressed. I must look right. I wish Heppi were here to help me.

7

February 16

DADDY HAS FIFTEEN acres all in March corn.
And today he is out riding around to see to his
fencing with one of the hands. Mama is paying
calls. And I? I did not sleep all night. I have a
strange sort of headache. Mama has given me
some laudanum, and I am supposed to be resting, but I am writing instead.

Last evening Rene asked me to marry him. We had supper and nothing was said. Indeed, conversation seemed to be only between Daddy and Rene. It was about the production of cotton. "Isn't it funny," Rene said, "that I deal in silk and you deal in cotton?"

Then, sensing that Mama and I were left out, he started to tell us about New York and the places you could go. He told us about the Keith Hippodrome, soon to open, where he hoped to see Harry Houdini, and Hammerstein's Roof Garden. "I've been to most places," he told us, "but the place I've never been is to the salt marshes and sand dunes at the end of our trolley line. I've always wanted to take a picnic lunch there with someone."

After supper Mama and Daddy left us alone in the parlor.

"You know, I've asked your father for your hand," he said to me.

I said yes, I knew.

"I know I'm twice your age, Rose. But a lot of marriages are like that. I know in many ways you are still a child, yet in so many others you are an enchanting young lady. If you marry me, I promise to honor both those qualities in you."

I didn't want to look into his blue eyes. For I knew I would be lost if I did.

"I know you don't love me. I don't expect you to in the beginning. I hope to earn that love. I know I must."

I said nothing.

"But I love you. You should know that. I want to give you time, of course. I know you need more time."

He had thrown me a lifeline! "Yes, please, give me some time to think on it. It's all so new to me."

He had taken my hand and now he released it and tucked my hair on the left side behind my ear. "I fell in love with you the first time I saw you, Rose."

He was breaking my heart, the way he spoke, surely. I smiled at him. Is it possible to be so attracted to a man and not love him? Is that what love is? Attraction? No, I think it goes deeper than that, but how, I don't know yet.

He smiled at me, and something inside me fell. And then he sat down to play the piano, and my mother and father came into the room. He played Chopin and some popular songs.

How is one supposed to know? Oh, I wish Heppi were here. She would tell me.

February 19

BACK IN SCHOOL. I couldn't concentrate today and I felt Amelia's eyes on me constantly, as if she knew something. And as it turned out, she does.

Oh, now I am more confused. Now I really need advice.

At lunchtime Amelia took me aside, grinning snidely. "Did he ask you yet?" she prodded.

Oh, this girl! Is there anything she doesn't know? Do her parents let her hear everything? And how did they know Rene asked for my hand?

"Yes," I breathed miserably.

"And what are you going to do?"

"Say no."

"No? You can't say no. Haven't your parents told you anything?"

More here than meets the eyes. I asked her what she meant. And she told me. Oh, how I wish she hadn't told me.

"Your father's financial affairs are in a terrible state. That's what my father says. Rene has money, lots of it, and he wants to help. So he now holds the mortgage on your father's whole plantation."

Well, I didn't know whether to spit in her face or hug her for letting me in on things. But the world swam in front of my eyes. So that is why Daddy and Mama want me to marry him. Because he owns them, lock, stock, and barrel.

Right then and there I threw up in the corner of the school yard. I must say, Amelia played the part of a good friend. She held my forehead as I leaned over, she gave me her good handkerchief to wipe my mouth, and she advised me. For once I was glad of her sharpness and her daring.

"What are you going to do?" she asked again.

"I don't know."

"Well, let me tell you one thing. Don't let all this business talk interfere with your decision. He's a good catch. And if you love him in the least little bit, you should say yes. But if you do—and this is important—if you do, don't let him know you know he holds all your father's financial interests. And don't let your father know you know, either. If you can't do that, you should say no to him."

She is right, of course. Oh, why can't I think like her? She was nodding her head at me. "Just say yes, if you want, and go along for the ride," she said. "If you think you can love him. Don't let this men's nonsense ruin things for you. My father sees this kind of nonsense all the time. Men always sort it out, and we women shouldn't be concerned."

Oh, if only I could be as hard as she is. But every time I think of Rene, now, I think of him owning my daddy. How could I love him with anything like that in mind?

We walked back to the school door. Amelia held my arm. "Think of it this way," she said, "maybe it's a good thing he owns your daddy's interests rather than somebody else who could decide at any minute to fore-close on the mortgage and leave you all with nothing. Did you ever think of that?"

No, I hadn't. But, then, what about this? If I say no, will Rene foreclose on the mortgage? Is that why Mama and Daddy want me to marry him? Oh, I can't bear the thought of it. Am I just a bargaining chip, then, in their lives?

Rene has asked me to make up my mind within the month. He must return to New York soon, he says. Oh, I wish I had never been born!

⊛

AT SUPPER neither Mama nor Daddy spoke of the matter at all. All Daddy spoke of is that President McKinley has announced that he is going to run again. And that this Saturday he and Rene are finally going to take their hunt-ing trip. I blushed at the sound of Rene's name and hoped they didn't see it. It is difficult being the only one at the supper table with them. If Heppi were here she would at least make conversation.

February 24

OH, THE MOST horrible thing has happened this day. Daddy and Rene almost drowned! They were going, by sailboat, to Rose Island on Broad River when a squall came up of a sudden. They were between Archers Creek and Rose Island. Before they could get down the foremast, the boat went bottom up and the two of them, along with two Negro helpers, were in the water. It was the most terrible storm, and they fought and fought to get the boat righted. It turned over twenty times on them, Daddy said, and when they had just about given up hope, it righted itself and Monday, who works for Daddy, got in and bailed out the water with his hat. When the storm abated, the others got in, cold and near drowned.

They had to paddle for two hours against wind and tide before reaching shore. At home here, with the onset of the storm, Mama was in a state of pure anxiety, I can put down here, thinking something like this had happened. Opal and I tried to becalm her, but she would have none of it and kept watching at the window, peering through the terrible gusting wind and lightning toward the dock at the end of our property.

When finally she saw their little boat approaching, she near exploded. I just about got a coat around her shoulders when she ran out to greet them, with blankets in hand. I took up another blanket and ran out, too, for I thought that I had lost Rene and my father both. What would we do? I agonized. Would the bank foreclose on our house? What would Mama and little Benjamin and I do?

It was in those terrible moments of watching at the front windows that I knew that I did not want to lose Rene. If he had been lost, something would have gone out of my life. Some chance, some challenge that had been given to me to help Mama and Daddy and little Benjamin. And I am, after all, fifteen years old. I am a woman. A child no longer. Rene has seen that in me. Why can't I see it in myself?

I will marry him. He has brought something into my life in the short time I've known him. Being on the same level as him and treated as an equal by him has done much for me. I like it.

I ran to him, on the dock, and he opened his arms to me and I allowed him, wet as he was, to hold me. I put the blanket around him, and all four of us walked back to the house.

Daddy says that without Rene they surely would have perished. "He knew what to do

every minute of the time. He was fearless,"
Daddy said. "He took charge. He personally
hauled me out of the water and into the boat. I
couldn't make it on my own."

I owe Rene a great debt. He saved Daddy.
But that isn't why I shall marry him. This in-
cident has made me see another side to him
that I hadn't seen before. And I like it.

8

February 25

THIS MORNING, with the harsh light of sun, I
have doubts again. What makes us love somebody? Guilt? Necessity? Is there a love that is
just pure love for the sake of one's heart?
Mama says I should not dwell on such questions, they are too large for a girl my age. We
talked quietly at breakfast while Daddy and

Rene slept. For Rene, of course, stayed over the night, coddled and cosseted by Mama as if he were her own.

We are all terribly shaken by what happened. Daddy personally gave thanks to God for saving him and Rene from a watery grave. And when they slept in this morning, it gave me a chance to think.

"If I wed Rene, suppose he is mean to me?" I asked Mama. She said we all take that chance, that nothing is guaranteed. "But what if I never come back here again?" I asked.

She said I should come back for the birth of my first child. For the birth of every child, and then in between. I blushed, thinking of children.

I then asked, "Do you think he's right for me?"

And Mama smiled. "He is definitely not wrong," she said. "And even if the answer lies somewhere in between, you will do well."

"I think I shall wed him," I told Mama calmly.

And she smiled back and said, "Good."

❀

MAMA HAS the answer to all my questions, but her answers don't mean anything. I am thinking that is what love is. Always having questions but never having the answer, and just keeping on trying to get it.

❀

RENE WAS the first up. He came downstairs, crisply attired in the whitest of shirts, his face freshly shaven, smelling of rose water and soap. Opal agreed to stay out of the kitchen so I could make him breakfast. The dining room table was set with a lace cloth and our good crystal and chinaware and candles.

As I set down his cup of coffee and lit the candles, he asked, "What's all this for?"

"In celebration of life," I told him.

He looked across the table at me and I at him. Then he held out his hand and I went around to him and took it.

"You've made your decision," he said.

I said yes, I had, and I was going to marry him.

"I had to nearly drown in order to get you to say yes," he teased. Then, without rising, he took me in his arms and I leaned down to kiss him. In the background I heard noises from the house, Opal and Mama talking, Benjamin chatting away somewhere, but I paid mind to none of it. It was as if the world had gone away. My first kiss. And he was so gentle it was like the touch of a butterfly's wing. I felt stirrings inside me that I had never felt before.

He sat me on his knee and looked at me with that fine light of intelligence in his eyes. "Are you sure? This isn't because of what happened yesterday?"

"Yes, it is," I said. "I almost lost you."

He kissed me again, more insistent this time, and I didn't want to pull away, but I had to jump up and see to the bacon and eggs I was making for him. My head was swimming. If this is what marriage will be like, I have no reason to fear.

I AM TO BE WED! I have given my heart and my life and my word to a man. I can scarce believe it. One minute I am dancing on air and the next I am terrified. But mostly I am flattered and feel important, like Queen Victoria. When Daddy heard, he insisted on breaking open a bottle of champagne for lunch! And he and Mama toasted us. Rene held my hand and I was allowed half a glass of champagne. Imagine! I am to be married, but I can't have a full glass of champagne! Rene and I laughed over that. Oh, his teeth are so white, and I am so glad he has a sense of humor.

Oh, someone has just arrived. We are expecting the return of Heppi and Josh.

It is them! I must go downstairs.

9

February 25 (continued)

HEPPI AND JOSH look wonderful. Heppi has a light in her eyes I have never seen before and she looks in full bloom. If that is what marriage does to you, I am glad I said yes. She can scarce believe Rene and I are to be wed, and she kissed us both and said she was hoping for us.

"When will it be?" she asked. I told her

Rene wanted to wed before he leaves at the end of next month, but I didn't know if we could get a wedding together by then. She offered to help. She kissed me and said she'd miss me. I know I shall miss her.

February 26

MY WEDDING DATE is March 27, and like Heppi, I shall be wed here at home in the parlor. Oh, Mama is ecstatic. And I am glad I can make her happy. She so deserves to be free of worry. But am I marrying Rene for my parents or for myself? Is there any difference? If there is, I am afraid to think on it. Because this isn't a dreadful thing I am doing and there are days I know I could love him.

There was talk about my wearing Heppi's wedding dress, to save time (and money?), but it is too large and Mama said I should have my own to give to my daughter when she weds.

My daughter! Oh, I can't think on it.

Right then and there, of course, Rene said he'd supply the silk, he hoped he could do that for his own wedding, at least. There was some talk about inviting his brother, but Adrian is in New York, running the business up there, and with Rene to be wed and not available for a while, he can't come.

So Josh will stand up for Rene, and Heppi, for me, of course.

February 27

BUT STILL, our daily life must go on. Today Daddy said he's going to soak the corn on the cob in salt water before giving it to the horses, because then they will eat the whole cob and he will need less corn. I wonder how much in debt he is. And I wonder, when I leave here, how I will miss these little (and big) decisions that keep the place going. I went to the barn today and told myself: I won't be able to just wander out here anymore. Rene has promised to ship my horse, Tom Jones, and his up north. Oh, I was so happy. I couldn't bear to leave Tom Jones! But my head got dizzy when I realized I'm leaving Mama and Daddy and Benjamin and everything else down here. And I'll soon be a Yankee. Oh, all my life, everyone I knew hated Yankees. And here I am marrying one.

I cannot even imagine what it will be like, leaving this place. I know no other life than this. How will I fare?

Mama is endlessly giving me advice about running a household, about hiring servants. But I told her likely Rene will do that. She said not to put too much on my husband but to take the reins in my own hands on occasion. "He'll appreciate it, you'll see," she promised.

March 3

YESTERDAY, Mama and Heppi and I went again to Beaufort to have me measured for a dress. Rene has gotten the silk for both of us, and Heppi is to wear rose, in honor of me. I felt like a fairy princess draped in my fabric. The mood at the dressmaker's was joyous one moment and tear-filled the next. Since Rene took us, he accompanied us to the hotel and to supper. He was there for us every moment we needed him. Mama says it is so nice to have another man in the family.

I HAVE BEEN skipping rope in my spare time here at home. Mama says it is good exercise, and I want to lose five pounds before my wedding. I can skip almost to a hundred jumps, and I was breathless and my hair disheveled when Rene rode up in the backyard on his horse, dismounted, and bade me stop. Then he handed me a small box. I knew what it was, of course. The ring for my betrothal. He slipped it on me, then and there, and kissed me. I ran into the house to show it to Mama.

There was a beautiful full moon last night. We all watched it from the front porch. Rene whispered in my ear that it meant good luck. In Chicago they have had a severe snowstorm that stopped everything. Rene says the city is at a standstill and railroad cars filled with cattle are stranded on Madison Street. I could see the businessman's concern in his face.

March 4

I SUPPOSE I shall have to invite Amelia to the wedding. After all, if she isn't the reason all this is happening, I can't think of another.

March 5

MAMA AND DADDY said I must continue on with school until I wed, with only one week off ahead of time. Last night Rene came to visit and brought some photographs of the house he owns in Brooklyn. It is a large Victorian, with porches and turrets and a wide lawn. The street it is on is called Dorchester Road, and it is a wide avenue with green in between the lanes and other large, lovely houses just like ours. Oh, I can't wait to explore this house. Rene says I may have whichever room I want for my own pursuits. Think of it! He has a house-keeper, and there will be maids and a gardener and a stable boy. Rene says there is a stable and carriage house out back. Oh, sometimes I am so frightened I want to hide under my covers and forget the whole thing. But I'm excited, too.

March 10

WE HAVE HAD dress fittings, and gone shopping, and had tea parties galore for everyone involved in the wedding. I feel as if I am on a skiff, drifting down the river. Speaking of rivers, Rene says our trip north will be by both boat and train. I shall have to sleep on the train. Will I be able to do that? I don't want to be a child and ruin everything for Rene.

March 13

TONIGHT AT SUPPER I caught Daddy watching me with such sadness in his eyes that I wanted to go over and put my arms around him and promise him I would never leave. Ever.

March 17

THE HANDS are finished planting the corn. Think of it. I will not be here when it is full grown. Today is Saint Patrick's Day and Daddy has his club dinner.

March 18

RENE HAS NOT been around much. Mama reminds me that he has to wind up his business here in Beaufort and Charleston before we go north. "He's a businessman," she said. "You have to let him do what he has to do, Rose." I miss him.

March 22

I HAD MY last day at school this week. The girls all crowded around me when we said good-bye, and I could hear the envy in their voices. I pretended to be superior and happy at leaving. But I was scared and knew I wanted to come back tomorrow.

Our banns have been announced in church, although we won't be married there. Rene is Catholic, being French, but he says he isn't serious about it, that he will embrace my religion, which is Episcopalian. The Reverend Framingham will wed us, same as he wed Heppi and Josh. And, oh, they have finally moved out into their own house in Beaufort. It is lovely and large, and beautifully refurbished. It is made of three hundred thousand Carolina-made bricks. They have been very busy moving in. Poor Mama. She has her girls going in two different ways. Well, at least we're not eating the bread of idleness.

We shall each be mistress of our own home and will look well to the ways of our household. And more than that, we won't be a worry to Mama and Daddy anymore.

I want to ask Heppi what she knows about Rene holding the mortgage on this place, and what my marriage will mean as far as that is concerned, but somehow I sense she would not want to speak of it. And then again, maybe she doesn't know, and I don't want to shock or sadden her. She is so happy.

Today she took me on a tour of their home. It has a wide, lovely center hall and two parlors and a dining room that overlooks the garden. It suits Heppi. I am happy for her.

March 26

IT IS VERY LATE, yet I can't sleep. Tonight we had a before-wedding dinner. Tomorrow I get married. The whole house is silent.

After dinner I slipped out of the house and walked down to the waterfront and looked back. It is the only home I have ever known. What will I do in Brooklyn in a house without a tabby foundation and strong pillars to hold it up? The wind off the water was persistent yet gentle, and blew some sand around my face. I breathed in the fragrance of it, even as I listened to the rattle of the palmetto trees out back and the ever-present sound of the tide behind me. Then I went back up behind the house to the barns. A single lantern burned inside. I told Jimmy I wanted to ride Tom Jones, so he saddled him for me and I took him out, over sand dunes and past the swampy places. I walked him very carefully past the twisted cedars and crooked pines behind the house, not going too far because it was dark by then. But I knew my way without seeing, and so did Tom Jones.

All this will be gone from me tomorrow. Will I be able to bear it? How will my world change? What does Brooklyn have to offer me?

I saw a lantern behind the house near the back door and knew it was Rene looking for me. I can't alarm him, I thought. So I let Tom Jones take me back to the barn. Rene was waiting there for me when we arrived, and he helped me off my horse, then held me.

"It'll be all right, Rose," he told me, holding me close. "You can come back whenever you want to."

He knew! Somehow that makes me feel better.

PART TWO

Brooklyn, New York

1900

10

April 1

I HAVE NOT, of course, been able to write in this journal for days. Now, here I am on a train, going east to New York because our boat ride took us inland. Rene had business with some men about shipments on the Erie Canal. We traveled the canal on a paddle steamer and had a suite of our own that was luxurious. At every turn there was good food and music. Of course Rene got the royal treatment. It is late and now he is in the bar having a drink and I am in my nightgown and robe, trying to write. The ride is really very smooth.

I shall be quick. My wedding day morning, Becky Sharp, one of Daddy's mares, dropped a foal. Daddy said it was good luck for our wedding, which took place that morning at eleven.

I got up early on my wedding day and dressed in my riding clothes and went out to the stables to have a ride on Tom Jones. The mist was on the river, and the place was quiet, except for Jimmy taking care of the horses in the barn.

So I was the first one to see the foal.

"Come to have a last ride about the place, eh?" Jimmy asked.

I told him I'd done that last night, that I just wanted to see things in the morning light. Still, it sounded so sad. But Tom Jones took me straightaway on our favorite paths. I did not even have to direct him. I only know that as we headed to the water that was gently lapping on the shore and I gazed out across the river, I felt a huge fist wrapped around my heart.

How can one be so sad and so happy at the same time?

I couldn't eat anything before the ceremony, but I joined the family at the table to tell them about the foal. Then we went out to see it.

All morning my head was in a buzz of excitement. I could scarce believe I was getting married. Rene kept giving me fond looks, and I found myself blushing. The wedding ceremony was early, eleven in the morning, because we had to get started on our trip. I remember going about the house and telling myself: This is the last time I'll see this, and the last time I'll do that. Oh, it was terrible sad.

Heppi helped me to dress. I don't remember a bit of it. Everything seemed blurred and moving too fast. I know I said the right words for the reverend, that Mama cried and Daddy insisted everyone have champagne immediately afterward. Then everyone kissed and we sat down to a scrumptious wedding brunch. I know I looked beautiful in my silk gown. Little Benjamin acted as the ring bearer, and I cried when I saw him.

When I left, I hugged Mama and Daddy as if I were going to stay at a friend's overnight. I think tears were coming down my face, but Rene was right there for me, holding my arm and guiding me through the whole thing. His presence is such a comfort.

When I kissed Heppi good-bye, she whispered in my ear, "Remember, trust and love." And now here it is five days later and I understand what she meant.

At first I was scared, going off with a man

alone, but then Rene was very tender and loving with me. I found myself looking to him for
everything, clinging to him in strange places,
and he was there for me.

So it was not difficult for me to give myself
to him on our wedding night. And now we
have a different kind of closeness, to add to the
other.

I have noticed on our trip that the farther
north we go, the colder it gets. Rene warned
me of that, and so I have brought my warmer
clothing. Oh, everyone we meet is so nice to
me, and I am so proud to be introduced as his
bride. I want to be a good wife and please him,
and I hope I can.

April 3

WE HAVE ARRIVED in New York City! Oh,
what sights! Never did I ever hope to see so
many people in one place. The carriages! The

restaurants! The lights! The noise! I stayed close to Rene, believe me. He took me to a restaurant called Delmonico's for a late supper. We will stay overnight in this very fancy hotel, and I have felt, this whole time, as if I am living in a fairy tale.

April 6

RENE HAD SOME meetings with business associates in the dining room of the hotel yesterday, and so we didn't get started until nearly three. We came across the Brooklyn Bridge in our carriage. Rene wrapped me in a rug because it was very cold and told me the story of the bridge's construction. Oh, I wish Daddy could see it. But I get ahead of myself. I must tell of our homecoming first, and it was so bizarre I hesitate to write it, but I have promised always to tell the truth in my journal.

First, it was dark when we got to Dorchester Road, although there were streetlights and some lights on in neighboring houses. But not a one in our house. Rene was upset when he saw this. "I told her we'd be here this evening," he muttered. And when I asked him who, he said the housekeeper, Mrs. Kerwin. Then he paid the driver, who got our luggage onto the front walk and drove off. Rene found the front door key in his pocket, and we went up the steps.

The door was locked.

He opened it and we went in. I stayed behind him, because he knew the place and I didn't. We went through the center hall and Rene went about putting on lights. When he saw that the sofas and chairs were still covered with sheets, he muttered a curse.

"I told that woman we'd be here this day. Now why isn't the place in order?"

The large, empty house looked forbidding. Rene told me to sit down on one of the covered couches and keep my coat on, he was going downstairs to start the furnace. I waited while he did so. Outside, under the space of light from the nearest streetlight, I saw snow coming down. In April! What kind of a place is this Brooklyn?

Rene soon came upstairs, brushing his hands against each other. "Well, we'll have heat at least," he said. "Now, Mrs. Dumarest, will you require a cup of hot tea or do you wish to go to bed?"

I told him I was exhausted, and we turned out the lights downstairs and found our way up to the main bedroom. There, too, sheets covered everything, and when Rene pulled one off the bed we found it unmade.

Another muttered curse. "Now we'll have to find the linens," he said dismally.

"I think I saw a linen closet in the hall." I went out to look, was right, and found linens for the bed. Then, together, Rene and I made up the bed. We worked well together and I enjoyed that. "The bathroom is down the hall," he said. "I had it modernized. I'll turn on the lights for you."

My first night in my new home. Long after I knew that Rene was asleep beside me, I lay awake. Out the window, I could see the snow under the streetlights. From somewhere a clock was ticking. I snuggled close to Rene, feeling safe and secure and not at all afraid.

THIS MORNING I awoke to the *clip-clip-clop*ping of a horse and wagon on the street outside. I sat up, careful not to wake Rene. It must be the man who delivered the milk. I had never seen a milkman before, and so I peeked out the window. Yes, there he was, coming up our front steps. I heard the clinking of the milk bottles, saw his horse and wagon. Then I had an idea. I'd make breakfast and bring it up to Rene in bed. I could make breakfast as well as any old housekeeper, couldn't I?

I put on my robe and slippers and crept downstairs. Now that it was daylight, of course, I could see what the place looked like.

The stairway was wide and made of dark polished wood with a heavy banister and a carved newel post. It led into the center hall, in which there was a mirrored coatrack and dark wainscoting and several oil paintings of people I didn't know. The glass on the double front doors was frosted and etched. To one side, at the bottom of the stairway, was the dining room, with the same dark woodwork and with cheery rose-and-white paper depicting country scenes. On the other side of the hall was the parlor I'd sat in last night, with all the furniture still covered with white sheets.

Well, I'd do that much today, anyway. I'd get the sheets off the furniture.

There were lots of end tables and lamps and plants, and in the parlor, a fireplace with a marble mantel. On the landing of the stairway was a stained-glass window, and the morning sun streamed in, casting colors on my face. I smiled, feeling blessed, and found my way through the hall and back to the kitchen.

It was there, next to the table in the center of the room, that I saw the woman lying on the floor. A bag of groceries was strewn about her.

I remember thinking: But I didn't hear anyone come in.

Then I thought: She is hurt. So I went to help her up.

I remember leaning over her and gasping. And then I heard someone scream. I put my hand over my mouth so I wouldn't scream and wished whoever it was would stop that screaming.

I was bent over, one hand over my mouth, the other across my stomach, crying, when Rene came up behind me. "Rose, what is it? What? Oh my God. Rose, step back; stop it, Rose; it's all right. I'm here."

I had been the one screaming. I looked at Rene, at his dear face. His hands were on my shoulders, and then he hugged me close for a moment. "Go into the parlor and sit down, child. I'll be along in a minute." His voice was so level, so sane.

I went, and waited. I heard him moving about there in the kitchen. "It's the housekeeper," he called out to me. "It's Mrs. Kerwin. She must have come yesterday and had a heart attack or something. I'm going to call the police."

I sat listening while he made the call from the telephone in the hall. We must get a phone at home, I thought crazily. Suppose Mama comes into the kitchen some morning and finds Opal dead on the floor?

Rene finished his call and came into the parlor. "Go upstairs and get dressed," he said softly. "They'll be here in a little while."

I nodded and got up. As I passed him, I saw him standing there, hands plunged into the pockets of his bathrobe. He was looking at the floor, scowling.

"I'm sorry I screamed," I said.

He looked at me and the light in his eyes was so intelligent and so loving that I didn't want to leave him at that moment. "Dear child," he said, "I'm sorry for such a first day in your new home." Then he kissed me, and I went upstairs to dress.

11

April 6 (continued)

RENE TOOK CHARGE this morning like he was President McKinley. He dressed in a wink, ran his hand over his face, determined there was no time to shave, and went downstairs before I had my petticoats on.

I saw him from the bedroom window. He went outside to the street, where there was a thin coating of snow, hailed a boy on a bicycle, pointed somewhere, drew some money out of his pocket, and I saw the boy go in the direction Rene had pointed. Then he was back in the house. And when I went downstairs he was in the kitchen, stirring up a fire in the top of the stove and putting a pot of coffee on.

All while the housekeeper lay on the floor. He stepped around her. I noticed he did not touch her, or the vegetables that were strewn on the floor around her.

I did not go in there. The front doorbell rang, and he dashed out to answer it.

It was the police in their tall helmets. Three of them. Rene ushered them in, introduced me, and brought them into the kitchen. There I heard him answering their questions about who he was and how he'd only recently taken ownership of the house and hired himself a housekeeper.

Then they came into the parlor and questioned me. Rene sat next to me on the couch while they asked me their whos and whys and whens. I was wide-eyed with fright. We had only two policemen in Beaufort, and they were both Negro. I'd never spoken to them. But I was brave and told these three everything I knew. Then they called for the coroner to have the body removed.

Before the coroner's wagon arrived, the boy Rene had given the money to came to the door and handed Rene a bag. I saw Rene tip him and thank him. Then he smiled at me. "Breakfast," he said. "Rolls, and I have coffee on. I'll get it; you don't have to go in there, Rose. Gentlemen, would you like coffee?"

How he could be so social with a dead body in the kitchen I don't know. But soon the coroner came, and while Rene and I drank coffee and ate buttered rolls in the parlor, they took Mrs. Kerwin outside and put her in the coroner's wagon.

"We may need you for further questioning," one of the policemen told Rene.

"We're here," he said. "This is our home."

Indeed. It is now, for all the horror of this first morning in it. We've come through our first crisis, and already I feel at home in the house. Like we've been through something together. And, of course, the same goes for Rene. We've come through together, and I've seen how he can take charge, and I feel even more confidence in him.

Confidence? Or love? Oh, I don't want to fall in love with him. Not yet. And maybe not ever. Still, I am feeling closer every day.

No, not love. It was his mood, his cheerful outlook, his firm resolve that got me through it all. I think I just may have myself the right husband.

April 7

WHEREVER RENE was supposed to go yesterday, he did not go. "I'll not leave you alone," he said. "I'm supposed to have not only a housekeeper but a man about the place, part body servant, part butler, and part indoor-outdoor man."

I smiled. He said I should just go about my business and unpack my things. He was expecting to interview his half-indoor, half-outdoor man this morning.

"I want to see the yard first," I told him. But I could not go through the kitchen. The police were coming back to examine it for any clues that might lead them to think there had been any foul play.

I went out the side door to a little porch, then down the steps and around to the back-yard.

There is a great deal of room out there, at

least an acre. A carriage house and stable for horses sits on the back of it. I went to inspect that first and saw there is ample room for our two horses when they come. There is a darling swing on a maple tree, plenty of rosebushes and rhododendrons, birdbaths, a gazebo, and some small statues of angels. There is a goldfish pond, too. Immediately I thought of little Benjamin and how the yard would delight him. They must come here. I must plan for them to visit.

There is a black wrought-iron fence around the yard, but the place has that neglected look that grounds get after winter and before spring sets in.

At home, in between fishing for drumfish, Daddy would have the hands planting peanuts already.

Then I noticed a patch of ground to the side of the stables. It had been hoed up and had the appearance of a garden. Clearly there were rows of something already planted.

Maybe the housekeeper had done it, I decided. Surely nobody else would.

Then Rene came around from the side of the house. "How do you like the yard?" he asked.

I told him I liked it fine. I was so proud of the way he looked in his striped shirt, neat trousers, suspenders, and tie. This is my husband, I said to myself with pride.

I showed him the garden, and he scowled. "Someone's been poking around here in my absence."

When I suggested the housekeeper, Mrs. Kerwin, he said no, he'd only hired her before he left. She was to do no yard work. And if I saw anybody poking about the yard, I was to tell him. He wanted no more trouble than he already had.

I said yes, I would. Then I asked him who had been feeding the goldfish. He said he had a boy coming round to do that, but the boy was far more interested in baseball than gardening, so it wasn't him. No, he said, he suspected an interloper.

April 10

WITHIN THE PAST few days, it seems, things have settled down. Rene hired the boy who fetched us breakfast that morning to help carry things about the house and put them in the right places. We have been eating our supper out, although I told Rene I can cook. He said no, he doesn't want me in the kitchen like that.

"You go in the kitchen to oversee things," he said, "like your mother does."

It touched me, his saying that. I know he respects Mama a lot. We ate at a lovely restaurant on Flatbush Avenue. Rene still needs a man about the place, a cook and housekeeper, and a washerwoman. He has ads in the *Brooklyn Eagle* for such.

I have taken all the sheets off the furniture, and on especially nice days, I air the house out. There are yellow daffodils in great plenty about the place, and I have picked some and put a vase in the front parlor and in Rene's study.

I make breakfast for Rene and am setting our bedroom to rights. The rest of our things have yet to be shipped north, so we don't have everything yet.

April 12

TODAY I MET the milkman. His name is Mr. Drayton, and his horse's name is Maybelle. I purchased some eggs and butter, also, remembering how Mama told me to take charge and not bother my husband about the little things.

And with some money Rene gave me, I walked down to the grocer on Flatbush Avenue and purchased some oranges, so I could squeeze juice for Rene for breakfast. We have a new icebox in the kitchen. I think it is wonderful.

I don't know what the rest of Brooklyn looks like, but Rene tells me some of it is still farmland. As far as the Dorchester Road part of it, it is lovely, with stately trees and neat walks and wide avenues and impressive homes. It is real country. It gives one a sense of peace and composure. Not like home, of course. I miss the water already. And the rattling of the palmetto trees. But I mustn't think of that. No, I must try to adjust to this place called Brooklyn.

12

April 12 (continued)

IT WILL BE Easter Sunday in a couple of days. I must plan an Easter dinner. At home we would have fresh fish that Daddy caught, turkey, and even wild duck. Oh, I mustn't think of home!

The police came back yesterday afternoon and told us that the housekeeper's death has been determined by the coroner to be caused by heart failure. Her husband came around to see us last evening and told Rene her funeral would be at the local Catholic church tomorrow. I told Rene we ought to go. He said he scarce knew the woman and didn't have the time.

I made breakfast for Rene this morning. I stumbled around the kitchen trying to find things while he was still asleep. But I managed to set the round table. I made eggs and bacon and coffee and toast. I burned my fingers on the black-top stove.

Reading the morning paper, Rene told me about the Baltimore and Ohio train line testing a train called the "Wind Splitter." It reaches speeds of more than 102 miles an hour. I wish I could take a train like that and go and see my family. But I didn't tell Rene that.

When I went to take his empty plate he put his arm around my waist and said my breakfast was excellent but that he didn't like the idea of my cooking. I told him I cooked at home a lot when the fancy seized me. He sat me on his lap then and said he'd hire us a cook soon. Then he kissed me and said how sorry he was that everything was so confused. We had a few moments like that, then he said he had to go. He was going to his office to settle some things this day. He said he'd take a hansom cab. Would I be all right here alone? I said I would. I'd keep busy. He kissed me and left.

Some people came around in answer to Rene's ads in the paper. But Rene directed me just to take names and addresses. So I did.

It was lonely without Rene. I miss the hustle and bustle of life at home, with always someone around. At noontime I made my lunch and took it out to the backyard.

It was then that I saw the girl.

She was just inside the wrought-iron fence at the side of the stable. And she was hoeing the garden. She seemed to be my age and was dressed in the plain, everyday clothes of the working class.

"Hello," I said.

She was startled and stopped hoeing to look at me. "Good mornin'," she answered, and I heard the Irish in her voice. She was a fine-looking girl, with a natural, healthy prettiness. Her reddish brown hair was tied back in a bun, but tendrils had broken loose and were hanging becomingly around her face.

"Who are you?"

"My name is Bridget. Bridget Moore."

"Did my husband hire you to do the gardening?" I knew this was not so, but after all, I am the mistress of this place, am I not? And I must be strong.

She shook her head no. "I was just after hoein' the weeds." Her face is full of freckles. I thought how we must sound, she with her Irish accent and me with my Southern drawl.

She said nobody had hired her.

Then what was she doing here? I asked. She blushed. Oh, she'd seen the ground, she told me, the beautiful earth begging for seed. And it looked almost as good as the earth used to look in Ireland. Before she came here. " 'Tis a shame to let it go to waste and not grow vegetables, ma'am," she said. "Good land is a gift from God."

I took exception to her telling me that. Like I didn't know. "I come from a plantation in South Carolina," I said. "My father grows cotton and peanuts and corn and everything. I know about land."

She did a little knee bob of a curtsy. "Meant no disrespect."

"What are you going to do with the vegetables?"

"Bring them home to my family. Himself went and got injured on the job. That's my pa. Ma is lookin' for work. We've got little ones to care for and my grandfather lives with us. He was in the war and ain't much good for anythin' now."

"I'll tell my husband and ask if you can keep the vegetables," I said. "I'll let you know. What kind of work does your mother do? And what about you? What do you do?"

"Ma's a good cook," she said. "I'll do anythin'."

That evening when Rene came home, I did ask him about her. We were getting ready to go out to dinner, at the house of some of his friends. It seems I had to be properly introduced as his wife.

I could see he didn't like any of it. "Why can't we hire her mother as cook?" I asked. "She's looking for work."

He shook his head no. "You can't just hire people we know nothing about," he said sternly. "They must be investigated, have references. They'll be in our home."

It was a reproach. Tears came to my eyes. Rene has a tower of steel inside him that you can't get around when he doesn't want you to. I have learned that. Now I must learn how to get around it.

Then he put his arm around me, softening. "If you see her tomorrow, tell her to come around. And bring her mother. I'll let her know about the job, and the vegetables."

April 14

THE WEATHER has been chilly and rainy. Not at all like spring at home. But Rene says that when the rain stops it will be lovely. Still, I'm disappointed. The only flowers that are out are crocuses and daffodils.

Yesterday we even had some snow. The paper said three inches. I felt sorry for the daffodils, who have their heads sticking out of it. Rene says they will survive.

I know Rene has his mind on a new shipment of silk that just came in. He told me how they have so many orders from Buffalo, where, he says, there are so many millionaires you can't count them on your fingers, and where they are all dressing their daughters to send to England to marry into nobility.

"What do they do with themselves, these millionaires?" I asked.

"Work," he said, "harder each day. Just like Adrian and I do."

We were having breakfast in the kitchen. He had the folded-up morning newspaper in one hand and was reading it while we talked. I was stunned. "Are you a millionaire?" I asked.

He took his eyes off the paper and smiled at me. "Yes, we are," he answered. "Though it is never to be spoken of."

"You and Adrian?" I asked.

"No," he said. "You and I. Adrian has his own resources."

I fell silent. Discussion of money only made me think of Mama and Daddy and home. Was part of his million our plantation?

"What do you do with your money?" I asked.

And he answered. "Invest. Tie it up in assets. But I hope to have a family and a good life, too. What is it, Rose? What's troubling you?"

"I don't like to talk about money."

"You shouldn't like it. Just depend on me and enjoy what we have."

Just then came a knock on the back door. It was Bridget, with her mother and what she called a Brooklyn cheesecake, which she'd made herself. Rene thanked her and gallantly offered them some breakfast, which they declined. He asked Bridget if she wanted to work for us as a helper and personal servant to me. Her eyes lit up. "Mama can cook," she said.

"I have no doubt that she can," Rene said, "but I must interview you both first and get some recommendations."

He brought them right into the parlor to interview them. I stayed in the kitchen, hoping they'd get the jobs. All Rene needed, he said, were some personal recommendations. Where did they live? As it turns out, they take the trolley line to get here. It's an Irish community where they live. Bridget told us the Irish have lived here in Brooklyn since the middle of the last century.

Rene said he'd have some of his people investigate them. It sounded so formal, even frightening. I wouldn't want anybody investigating me. Would they go into their neighborhood? He said yes, but not to worry about it. Just worry about what I was going to wear tonight, because we were invited out for supper.

April 15

WE HAD Easter dinner cooked by Mrs. Moore, Bridget's mother. It was a delicious ham with all the trimmings. Rene has decided to hire both of them. I am so glad.

13

April 20

THE SUN was bright and warm today and we have some tulips out now. The phone rang when Rene was out and it was Adrian, Rene's brother. We had a brief conversation. He asked me how his little brother was treating me, and I said fine. He invited us to his home for dinner. I said I would have Rene call him.

"The little bride," he called me. I wonder what Rene has told him about me. He sounds very nice.

Last night we went to the Willink House and Hotel on Flatbush Avenue for dinner with business friends of Rene's. He says the hotel is owned by two eccentric old ladies. We had an excellent supper, but I am tired of eating out, although I realize that many of these suppers are social obligations.

Still, I decided to make supper tonight for us, for we were supposed to be going out alone. I walked to Flatbush Avenue and went to the butcher and the greengrocer. Then I trudged home and made an excellent pot roast with vegetables and one of Grandmother's Connecticut pies. It was Mrs. Moore's day off.

Rene didn't know whether to be angry or pleased. "I don't want you slaving over a hot stove," he scolded. Yet he said the dinner was excellent, and I know he was pleased with my accomplishment. He hugged me and called me the "Mistress of Dorchester."

"Dorchester is the road, not the house," I reminded him.

"I think then that we'll name the house Dorchester," he said. "It sounds romantic, doesn't it?"

I said yes and asked him how you name a house. He said he didn't know, that you probably just referred to it that way. So we decided to call the house Dorchester. And Rene said I am the mistress.

He is happy with Bridget and her mother, Mrs. Moore. "We have to stop living like savages around here," he told me.

April 21

BRIDGET CAME this morning, bearing another Brooklyn cheesecake. "What would you have me do, sir?" she asked Rene. He told her just to keep his wife company, attend to her needs and wants, and help her mother.

"I can do all that and more, sir," she promised him. Then he kissed me and left. "Remember," he whispered in my ear, "you have a servant now. And remember you are the Mistress of Dorchester. Act accordingly."

"Of course I will," I promised.

"Not if I know you," he said. "If I know you, I'll come home and find you skipping rope with Bridget."

I must write to my mother. Other than a short note to let her know we arrived safely, I have not written.

April 22

TODAY WAS OUR DAY to go to supper at Rene's brother's house. They live near Bedford Avenue in the old William Payne house. It is a darling house with a front porch and lots of trees and a large front lawn on which they have a croquet set. Adrian is just as I thought, genial and protective of Rene, though he kids him a lot. His wife, Sara, is sweet and childlike in the way women get when they don't have children. I think we can be friends. She told me I must join the local flower club, that I would enjoy it. I said I would consider it. Afterward, when the men went into Adrian's study to have their smokes and drinks, she took me outside to show me her gardens. I think she is an accomplished married lady. I wish I could be like that.

April 29

RENE WENT to the local Episcopal church with me, even though he is supposed to be Catholic. He was sent to a school by his parents in France, he told me, where the priests were so strict that he left the church as soon as he attained his majority. Then he took me to New York to dine at Delmonico's. I missed my family dearly.

April 30

I HAVE A LETTER from Mama! How exciting! She tells of the lovely spring down there. Daddy has had his people plant seven acres of cotton. A dead porpoise, about eight feet long, washed up with the tide. Daddy secured a rope to it and dragged it onto the beach, and hopes to get about five gallons of oil out of it. Some cattle got into his corn and ate it badly. Little Benjamin has had a spring cold and is starting to say words. I must write, she says, and let her know about my new home. And, oh yes, Heppi is expecting a baby.

May 3

I ASKED RENE where he lived before he
bought this house. He said he rented part of
Dellwood House in Bay Ridge. He promised
to show it to me sometime. It is high on the
bluffs overlooking New York Bay and the
hills of Staten Island. But he had always
wanted his own home, and so he purchased
this one right before his trip when he met me.
Rene doesn't say much about his past, or his
family, with the exception of Adrian. It oc-
curred to me today that he has told me nothing. I wonder why. Did he tell my parents?
He must have told Daddy something, or
Daddy would never want me to marry him.
Suppose he comes from people who are
wanted by the law back in France? Suppose
he owes great globs of money? Oh, I must
stop being so foolish.

May 10

AS THE WEATHER becomes nicer, I find it difficult to stay indoors. I am spending quite a bit of time outside, tending to the flowers. We have the most beautiful peonies behind the house. They are white and pale pink, full pink, and deep magenta. I can't stop looking at them.

May 17

TODAY RENE caught me weeding the garden, and so he immediately said he must hire a gardener, that he has been remiss. He put an ad in the *Brooklyn Eagle,* not only for a gardener but for an all-around man, and a washerwoman. Mrs. Moore has been kindly washing our clothes and putting them on the drying line out back.

May 19

TODAY I FOUND a beautiful black-and-white cat on the stoop in back of the house. He is most friendly. I told Rene I wanted to keep him, and he said all right, but don't be upset if someone comes around claiming him for their own. I think I shall name him Patches.

May 20

PATCHES IS doing quite well and nobody has yet claimed him. He sleeps at the foot of our bed at night. I think it is very decent of Rene to allow this, since he isn't overly fond of cats, but sometimes I think he would grant me just about anything I wanted. I know he spoils me. But I like it.

For instance, this morning I wanted to go walking on Dorchester Road, and since it was

Sunday, Rene agreed. And it was as if we came out of a beehive, Rene and I, because of a sudden we met all our neighbors.

Mrs. Manning lives next door. She is elderly with white hair and a glint in her eye. She is in a wheelchair and has a young black man wheel her about. "I see you outside all the time with the flowers," she said. "What are you going to do with all the flowers?"

I told her that where I come from, on Decoration Day, we gather flowers and take them to the cemeteries to put on the graves of the war dead. She asked me then if I had anybody who died in the war. I told her about my daddy's uncle Sumner, but that I didn't know him. She asked why I brought flowers to the cemetery then. "It doesn't matter if we know the person or not," I said. "We put flowers on all the graves."

Well, she thought that was the best idea since electricity came to Brooklyn. The neighbors here put flowers only on the graves of those they know, she told me, and the other graves look so lost and lonely. "Why don't you encourage the neighbors hereabouts to go with you and do the same thing?" she asked. "You know, here on Dorchester Road we have a big picnic, with speeches and everything, on Decoration Day. It could be part of the ceremonies."

I looked at Rene. "You could visit some neighbors," he said, "and have them pass the word. It's for a good cause."

So I said I would. Now what have I gotten myself into?

14

May 23

BRIDGET AND I literally knocked on doors this day, to solicit donors to bring flowers for Decoration Day. We knocked on the doors of Mrs. Mason, Mrs. Dell, and Mrs. Norwich. They all liked the idea of bringing flowers to the grave sites of the war dead. Then we had to visit the two churches involved, the Catholic and the Episcopalian, to see if there are any graves of war veterans. It turns out there are. And we went to make a count so we would have enough flowers.

May 30

TODAY IS Decoration Day, and the weather was beautiful. Mrs. Moore made up a ham and a platter of potato salad. Her potato salad is almost as good as Opal's. I put on my next-best dress (it is white) and a large hat, white gloves, and shoes, and we went to the festivities. Rene and I were introduced as newcomers. After the ceremonies and speeches, I assembled with the other women in back of the parade, each with a bouquet of flowers in our hands, and we walked to the cemeteries. Then we who had flowers went about distributing them on the graves. How pretty they looked! I heard Mrs. Norwich say we should do this every year.

Rene said I had started something. And if he wasn't busy calling me the Mistress of Dorchester, he would call me Elizabeth Cady Stanton. She's the woman who went about talking of women's rights.

June 1

RENE TOLD ME of a train wreck that happened in Mississippi on the Illinois Central Railroad. An engineer named Casey Jones was killed. The name of the train was the Cannonball Express. The papers said Jones couldn't read the signal lights because of the dense fog.

I love it when Rene reads to me from the newspapers at breakfast, because then we discuss things. He seems to value my opinions.

Another item from today's papers was about the reunion of forty thousand veterans of the Confederate Army in Louisville, Ken-

tucky. We both marveled that there were so
many vets left on either side.

June 7

TODAY I WATCHED Rene play tennis. He belongs to the Knickerbocker Field Club on East
18th Street, here in Brooklyn. He says we
must soon go to a club supper, next time they
have one.

June 10

RENE HAS HIRED a washerwoman and a gardener. They both seem very capable.

June 15

I WENT TO the greengrocer and the butcher
with Bridget today. We purchased some very

nice lamb chops and potatoes and vegetables, and when I came home I showed Bridget how to make a Connecticut pie.

At the butcher's we met a very nice young man named Charley. He was carrying haunches of beef in from the delivery wagon, and the butcher scolded him without mercy because he dropped a haunch of beef on the sawdust floor. I felt so sorry for him. When we were ready to leave, the butcher assigned Charley the task of carrying our bundles home. We had a nice conversation with him. I know Rene tells me not to be so familiar with the servants, but we are all human beings, aren't we?

It turns out that Charley is helping to support his family. And he is looking for another job, and I thought immediately of the all-around man that Rene needs. So at supper I told him about Charley.

"Rose," he said, "you can't hire all of Flatbush."

I said I know and managed to look sufficiently crestfallen so that he took my hand. "I'll see him if he comes," he said. "Have Bridget send him around."

Bridget got word to him. He comes tomorrow.

June 20

A LOT HAS happened. Another letter came from home. My family is going to stay on the plantation this summer, though they usually go inland to escape the fevers from the swamps. I think Daddy wants to save money. Some servants have gathered plums, and Mama is overseeing the making of plum jam. Heppi is doing well, and she and Josh visit home frequently. Little Benjamin is saying more words and has taken to sitting in the kitchen and banging pots and pans.

I wrote back immediately, of course, and

told them about my adventures on Decoration Day.

Charley came over to see Rene about the job. They were a long time in Rene's study, and for a while I stood outside the door and listened.

I heard Rene tell him he needed somebody he could depend on, who could be counted on in any emergency, who could live on the third floor, be available to drive the carriage, attend to his needs, and, when around, answer the door. And did he know horses?

I crept away as Charley said yes, he could handle horses as well.

Rene hired him. So now we have five servants.

June 24

WE HAVE beautiful roses, both in front of the house and in back. The gardener, whose name is Joseph, knows a lot about flowers and lawn care. He comes twice a week, and Rene told me I am to tell him what I want with the flowers. The first thing I wanted was window boxes, like we have at home, so he made some and put them in front and on the side of the house. They look lovely.

June 27

THIS EVENING we went to a supper at the Knickerbocker Club. Although it is men only, the women are invited for social occasions. I was much impressed with their clubhouse and their dining room. At home, Daddy belongs to a club, so I am quite accustomed to it.

June 30

TODAY A VERY large delivery-wagon-type vehicle pulled up in front of our house. In it were

our horses. They arrived at the docks yesterday, having come by steamboat. Tom Jones
was glad to see me, and I, him. With him was
the mare Rene had bought from Daddy in
what seems so long ago now. Can it be that
six months ago I'd just met Rene? It seems
impossible.

July 5

YESTERDAY, EARLY, I awoke and crept downstairs, where I knew Mrs. Moore was making a
picnic lunch for us. I came up with the idea
two days ago. I would make a picnic lunch and
go with Rene to the end of our trolley line,
where the salt marshes are. He always wanted
to picnic there.

When I saw that the lunch was all packed,
I went back upstairs and awoke him for break-
fast and wished him a happy Fourth of July.
Then I told him what I had planned. He smiled

and said he'd love to go. "Nobody has ever thought to do anything like that for me before," he said.

There is an underlying sadness in Rene, which I cannot figure out. Is it the reason he does not speak of his past? To think that he has all this money and all this authority, and yet he seems sad. I wonder if I shall ever find out why.

15

July 5 (continued)

ANYWAY, the picnic was a huge success. I am so glad I thought of it. Rene and I sat on a blanket on the sand dunes and watched the water and the gulls and had quite an afternoon of it, all by ourselves. We watched fireworks in the distance at the end of the day, then caught the last trolley back home.

July 10

I NEVER recorded it here, but Rene allowed
Bridget to keep the contents of her garden for
her family. That is Rene. He is stern and sometimes seems very stiff-necked, yet under it all
he has a kindness that he doesn't like to bandy
about.

July 12

I HAVE NOT yet ridden Tom Jones, although
I have taken him around the yard. Rene says
he hopes I'll wait for when he can ride his
Peaches. But he has had Tom Jones out and
says the horse absolutely cannot abide Mr.
Ford's horseless carriage, and we must be very
careful of him in the streets.

July 17

BRIDGET HAS told me that her maternal
grandfather was killed in the draft riots of '63.

How terrible. I told her I thought the riots were the mayor's fault, because he sent all the city's police and soldiers to Gettysburg to fight and left the city defenseless. Bridget says I have a lot of opinions for a woman, and I told her that back home we were all expected to have opinions, that I'm not the little Southern belle with nothing but honeysuckle for brains.

Then she told me about her father's father, who fought in the war. She says that although he is crippled he can still carve the most beautiful things out of wood. I asked what and she said anything. Rene's birthday is coming up soon and maybe I will get him something Bridget's grandfather has carved. But first I will have to go and pick it out.

July 20

MRS. MOORE doesn't approve of my going into their neighborhood. "Now, Bridget," she said, "why would you be wantin' to take this child to where we live? You know she's quality and don't belong there." But I want to go.

July 27

TODAY RENE took me shopping in New York. Charley drove the barouche, which is dark blue trimmed with black. He had it nicely polished. We went to Simpson-Crawford on Sixth Avenue, where I bought some fall dresses, new underthings, shoes, and a long skirt and middy blouse and a robe. After that Rene took me to lunch on Ninth Avenue and University Place, where we had French food. Rene drank French wine but ordered none for me because, he said, it was too hot outside and I wasn't accustomed to it.

I think I could almost love Rene. And this I did not plan on. I planned just to marry him because he is nice and has position and garners esteem. And because he holds the mortgage on Daddy's plantation. I really did it for Mama and Daddy, if I were to be honest. The thing I need to know is, why won't he speak of his family? And why does he seem to have such a sadness in him?

Tomorrow I go with Bridget into her neighborhood.

July 28

IT IS VERY HOT. Rene told me at breakfast that he wants to take me to the mountains for a vacation. But I said no. The house is cool, I have everything I need right here, and if I want to go anywhere, I'd go home. He just shrugged. I hope I haven't hurt his feelings.

I was gone all afternoon with Bridget. We took the trolley for what seemed like endless blocks, west of here into her neighborhood. I wish I hadn't gone. It is all a series of run-down houses, some that never saw a coat of paint, ragged children playing in the middle of the horse dung and urine in the streets, and garbage falling out of boxes. And the smell is horrible. So many houses had broken or cracked windows, and since the day was nice, the front doors all stood open.

But most of all the place reeked of failure, desolation, and despair. Dingy laundry ran on lines across the streets; vendors were everywhere. When we got off the trolley and Bridget showed me her house—which was at the end of the street and at least had an empty field next to it—it looked a little better than the others. But still it is in sad repair. She introduced me to two men sitting in the front yard. One was her injured father and the other his father. I shook their hands. Her grandfather must be in his eighties. He showed me the things he'd carved. One I particularly liked. It was a carved pipe stand, and I thought how perfect it would be for Rene's pipes. So I bought it and we got on the trolley and came back home.

The only trouble was that when we got home, Rene was there, having left work early. I was glad I had the pipe stand in a bag. "Where have you been?" he asked. When I told him, he scowled and called Bridget into his study. "If you take her there again, I shall terminate your services," I heard him scolding her. But he said nothing to me and I felt like a child. Oh, I feel so badly for Bridget.

"That man really loves you," Bridget said, as she started to set the table for supper.

But I didn't care. I went into the study, where he was reading the mail behind his desk. "Tell me if you don't want me going someplace," I said. "Don't make me feel like a child, between you and Bridget."

He smiled. "You want me to scold you?"

"No."

"You want me to terminate your services?"

"I want you to discuss it with me," I said.

I saw respect in his eyes. "I wish you hadn't gone," he said. "It's a squalid place."

"Well, I should know about it. Doesn't anyone help the children?"

"We can't take them in, Rose. So don't start."

Still, I think somebody ought to be able to do something for them.

16

July 29

I HAVE SUSPECTED this for some time, but now I am sure. I am expecting a child! Oh, I am half afraid and all excited. I have written to Mama and she has written back saying it is likely so and that we should find a good doctor. But I haven't told Rene yet.

July 30

A NEIGHBOR came to call today. Her name is Mrs. Snelling and she lives in the large Victorian two doors down. It is three colors and ours is only two. Rene calls her house the Painted Lady.

I invited her in and had Bridget serve us tea, but Mrs. Snelling made no bones about her visit.

It seems she belongs to the Ladies of the Flatbush Branch of the Needlework Guild of America, one of the many women's organizations a lady can join in this neighborhood. And she was angry because I went over everybody's head to organize the trip to the cemeteries on Decoration Day.

"You've scarce been here a few months," she chided me. "Many of the ladies are angry with you that you didn't consult them."

I told her there hadn't been time.

She harrumphed and said that was not true. So I asked what the Needlework Guild of America did with the things they made.

"They are for charity," she said.

I told her about the poor Irish children in Bridget's neighborhood, and how they must suffer in winter for lack of warm clothes. "There is a case of charity for you," I finished.

She harrumphed again. "What have they done to deserve it?" she asked.

I told her nothing. I told her they hadn't done a single thing. And just maybe they had done some things not to deserve it. But that they were still a good cause.

"Tell you what, missy," she said, "you come to one of our meetings and tell the Ladies of Flatbush why we should do this. You convince them, and we'll make those children a project."

I thanked her and said I would consider the matter.

August 4

I WAS GOING to tell Rene about the baby, because today is his birthday. But then a letter came from, of all people, his mother! I didn't even know he had a mother. He has made no mention of her this whole time. I thought she had died.

He read me the letter at breakfast. She is coming to visit, it says, within the next two months. And to meet Rene's new wife. She will let us know when her ship is likely to drop anchor.

Rene didn't look too happy about the whole thing, so I asked him about her, and why he didn't tell me about her. "She has a chateau in Aubigny," he said, "as well as a town house in Paris. My father is dead. He died when Adrian and I were boys, and she sent us off to be schooled by the Jesuits so she could continue on with her life on a high social level. There's nothing more to tell, Rose."

But apparently there was, which made him so sad. Her name, he said, is Charlotte, and he supposed we should give her the large corner bedroom upstairs. And did I mind if she came?

"Of course not," I told him. And then I told him that Adrian and Sara were coming for supper that night. And I gave him his pipe stand, which he liked so much.

And then I gave him the bigger present. I told him about the child.

August 10

RENE IS ECSTATIC about the child. He treats me as if I will break. And he doesn't want me to ride Tom Jones. The doctor says that as long as I have always ridden I can still ride, for a sensible amount of time and in a sensible manner.

So today we went on the trolley lines to the sand dunes at the end and enjoyed an afternoon there. We spoke of which room will belong to the baby and what its name will be. Rene said Louis, after his father, if it is a boy. And I said Marcella, after my maternal grandmother, if it is a girl. We agreed.

I have had no morning sickness, no queasiness at all. I feel in perfect health.

August 16

BECAUSE I FEEL so well, Rene has allowed me to ride Tom Jones up and down Dorchester Road at a leisurely pace. Oh, it is so good to go out on Tom Jones again. The smell of him, of the tack, the whole idea of riding again transports me back home, and if I close my eyes I am on the sand dunes at home again, where the tide comes in and out twice a day.

I met a few people I know on my ride and some I didn't know. One of those was an elderly man who was crossing Dorchester Road right in front of me. He fell, and I got down from Tom Jones to see if he was all right.

He said, "Thank you, missy. The old bones aren't what they used to be when I fought at Gettysburg."

He had a Southern accent!

I helped him onto the sidewalk, then took hold of Tom Jones's bridle and led them both to the man's house. He said his name was Mr. Cutler, and, yes, he'd fought at Gettysburg, on the side of the South.

He seemed rather sad, so I asked him if he was hurt. "Only my feelings," he said, "because my daughter won't allow me to go to see my family down South. Says we don't have the money, when I know we do. Oh, I shouldn't tell you my troubles, missy."

We talked a bit more, and then I saw him into the house.

August 22

WHAT A DAY! Today I went to speak to the Needlework Guild. It was an afternoon meeting held at Mrs. Snelling's house. When I arrived, she introduced me as the new neighbor, and quite a few of them called me "child." I feel that my Southern accent put off the rest of them, but for the most part they were polite.

At first they just had their business meeting. And when the president asked, "Any new business?" Mrs. Snelling got up and told them about me. How I was the one who organized the flower brigade on Decoration Day and, as if that weren't enough, I was now asking why they couldn't knit and make clothing for the Irish children who lived in the next neighborhood.

Then I got up there. Oh, so many faces, all staring at me. I couldn't work my voice at first, but then I thought of those children and what life would be like for them in the winter, and I forgot my own troubles and asked them to take my suggestion under consideration.

At first there was silence while they all stared at me. I heard one woman whisper to another, "How old is she? She looks like my Janey."

There were more whisperings. Then they started asking me questions. Personal and about the Irish children. They all knew by now that I was married to Rene Dumarest, and I know that brought me esteem. Several remarked on our house and the flowers.

Mrs. Snelling told me to sit down and have tea, that they would discuss the matter. And so I did. And before the afternoon was over, they said they would give me an answer in the near future.

Well, my part is over in all of this, I think. But they have made me feel so like a child begging for cookies, so unworthy of their consideration.

August 25

I HAVE FOUND out that besides this Needlework Guild there is a Ladies Book Club here on Dorchester Road, and Mrs. Snelling belongs to it, as well. Oh, I would love to belong to the book club. Imagine, reading books and discussing them with other women! I think I shall ask Mrs. Snelling if I may belong.

August 30

RENE IS HAVING the upstairs corner bedroom painted and repapered for his mother's visit. I picked out the paper. The room will be blue and white.

17

August 31

TODAY RENE came home all disheveled and with a cut on one cheekbone. I was so frightened. When I was cleaning off his face, I asked him what happened. He said there had been riots in the city this day, set off when a policeman got into a scuffle with a black man on a trolley car. Soon the fight got out of hand and every trolley car was stopped and every black man aboard dragged out and beaten. While I applied a remedy to his face, I asked him what he was doing uptown. He said he had business there. "You were on a trolley?" I asked. Because I knew he had asked Charley to stay the day at the dock. "No," he said, "but I got into a scuffle when they were beating a black man near to death."

He'd defended the black man, it turned out.

"I think," he confessed to me sheepishly later, "that my picture might be in the paper tomorrow. The photographers were there."

I thought of Opal and our people back home and I was so proud of what he'd done, and told him so.

September 1

WELL, RENE's picture is in the paper. It isn't the first time. The press knows who he is and

watches him. This picture showed him on the
ground, with Charley about to help him up.
And the headline read: "Wealthy businessman
comes to aid of Negro."

Rene wouldn't talk about it.

September 7

IT TURNED OUT somebody else would talk
about it, though. Yesterday there was a knock
on my side door, and there was Mrs. Snelling
with the paper in her hands. She all but shook
it in my face, saying, "We don't need this kind
of publicity in our neighborhood. I don't
know where you come from, miss, but we're
quiet, decent people here."

I told her there was nothing indecent about
the way Rene had come to the aid of the black
man. And she said that was a matter of opinion, and most in the neighborhood held to the
opinion that it was. Then she left.

I would never have thought I would allow a woman as stupid and prejudiced as her to upset me, but when she left, I cried. I know I am right and that Rene was right, but that doesn't help me feel any better. I can't understand why she doesn't like me.

September 8

I AM TRYING to focus on other things. I did not tell Rene about Mrs. Snelling's visit. So when he asked me why I was upset, I told him that the new fall dresses we purchased won't fit me come fall. But Rene says don't worry, I could wear a sack and he'd love me. Still, I must now go out and purchase special ones.

September 10

THE NEEDLEWORK GUILD sent a note around today saying they would take my suggestion to knit and sew clothing for the little Irish children for this winter. Oh, how good I feel! And more good news. The room for Rene's mother is finished. It looks lovely and now only needs a new bedcover and curtains, which Bridget and I will shop for soon. I worry about Rene's mother coming. Suppose she doesn't like me? Suppose she is like Mrs. Snelling?

September 17

THE DAYS ARE so lovely and the gardener has planted mums and other fall flowers that are now blooming. I can't bear to say good-bye to my gardens in the fall.

September 20

THERE DOESN'T seem to be much time to write in my journal anymore. I am so busy.

But I am determined to keep up with it. I went shopping again, with Bridget this time, to get some dresses to wear in the fall and winter before I have the baby. I am sewing a layette for him (or her), and Rene scolds because I am working too hard on it. He says I will ruin my eyes. I must oversee the fall cleaning.

September 25

I WAS SO HURT today. Mrs. Snelling called to tell me that the Ladies Book Club denied me membership. When I asked why, she said it is because I am too young. They don't think I can contribute anything of value. Well, I cried, I can tell you. Rene caught me crying and asked me what was wrong, and I told him.

"Well, tell them you don't want them," he said. Then he said something else, which makes me feel he knows so much that I don't know. "Someday, when you meet one of those hens from the book club, you ought to ask, face-to-face, if you are old enough yet. And I'll bet they never rejected you. I'll bet Mrs. Snelling took it on herself to reject you. Did you ever think it possible that the woman just plain doesn't like you, Rose?"

He came so close to the truth that I was afraid to look him in the face. But I truly never thought of it that way. I'm glad Rene is around to put another light on things.

September 27

THE BASEBALL TEAM by the name of the Brooklyn Dodgers has won something called the Pennant in the National League. Rene says he has seen them play and that next season he will take me to see one of their games.

October 1

WHAT BEAUTIFUL weather! In a place called Kitty Hawk, in North Carolina, two brothers by the name of Orville and Wilbur Wright are conducting experiments so man can fly, the newspapers say. I asked Rene if he would ever fly in one of their machines. "If it helped me to get around faster, of course," he said.

I can't imagine man flying. I don't think anybody else can, either. But, then, we could never imagine the horseless carriage, either, could we?

October 3

TODAY MRS. SNELLING and two other ladies came to the front door. I invited them in. They said they were organizing a committee against Negro ruffians. I told them we didn't have any around here, and they said they wanted to be prepared. "What is this committee going to do?" I asked. They said it will keep the members apprised of what is going on with the Negroes in New York City. They wanted me to sign their document, but I wouldn't do it.

Well, I lost my temper, I'm afraid. I told them I'm from the South and I don't have the feelings of discrimination against Negroes that they have. "We live with the Gullahs," I told them, "and we have no bad feelings about them."

I asked them why they didn't do something worthwhile with their time. They asked me, "Like what?" And I told them about Mr. Cutler, who wanted to go south to his family. "Help a Rebel?" they said, and they smirked. "That's like asking us to help a Negro." I said yes, it likely was. But that the war was long since over and he was old and incapacitated and it would make him happy. "Why don't you take it up with the Needlework Guild?" they asked me. "They've taken to listening to you."

I told them I probably would.

They left, all in a sniff. When I told Rene after he got home, he said I did the right thing and he was proud of me.

October 4

RENE WANTS to take me on a cruise up the Hudson River before the fall really sets in. I said I would love to go, but it will have to be soon, before I start to really look as if I am having a baby, because it isn't proper for a woman to bandy herself about when she is in my condition.

Rene says I should be proud of my condition. Which I am. The cruise is on a paddle steamer all the way up to Albany, where we will stay the night! There is music and entertainment, and we will have a parlor suite. We go in a week.

October 7

I DON'T KNOW whether it is the beauty of the fall days or the fact that I am nesting, but the house seems to have fallen into a rhythm that pleases me very much these days. I used to get up early, but now I sleep a little later. Rene is always up when I open my eyes. Usually he is already shaving in the bathroom or having breakfast downstairs. If it is a nice day, our bedroom is filled with sunshine and that pleases me. I put on a pretty robe and go downstairs. If Rene is at the table, I join him for coffee, and Mrs. Moore brings in my breakfast, which I enjoy with my husband.

When he leaves for work, I go into the kitchen to talk to the servants. I confer with them about what must be done this day.

Charley will have left with Rene, so there is usually only Mrs. Moore and Bridget. First to be decided upon is meals. If Rene and I are eating in, I plan supper, and either I plan to shop with Bridget or Mrs. Moore does. It is great fun, especially planning dessert. Then it is up to me to decide what else is to be done this day and we go over that. I am truly beginning to feel like I am mistress of this place and to appreciate what Mama does at home.

Afterward I may have another cup of coffee and read the papers on my own. Then I dress. Bridget may help if I am going out. Then I visit Tom Jones in the stable, to give him some sugar. If Charley is around he'll exercise him. Rene doesn't like me riding now that I'm very much pregnant. I come back inside to go over invitations, or answer some, and write to Mama or Heppi.

Then I take some kind of exercise, most likely a walk before lunch. In the afternoons I make calls or read. I must say I am turning into a full-fledged matron. These days I've been napping before Rene gets home, or fooling with my flowers. Or overseeing the supper. Watching Mama do these things for years has taught me much about how to be a lady.

I have to pay another visit to the Needlework Guild to ask them if they will sponsor Mr. Cutler on his visit south. I am not looking forward to it, but who knows? They may agree. It seems to me sometimes that they are only looking for decent causes to sponsor, and if they got about more and mixed with the rest of society, they might find some.

18

October 10

TODAY I WENT to see the Needlework Guild
again. I was invited in to their meeting. They
proudly showed me the clothing they are making for the Irish children. I must say it is all very
beautiful, from the knitted wear to the lovely
little homemade dresses and boys' trousers.

I thanked the ladies, one by one. They said

the clothing would likely be ready by Thanksgiving. Then I apologized and said I had another favor to ask them, and I told them about Mr. Cutler. Well, they listened intently and several said they knew of him but didn't know he'd fought at Gettysburg. And did he need anything else, perhaps? Some knitted caps or gloves for the winter? I told them no, thanking them for their kindness, and they said they'd need about a week to raise money for him to go south on the trains.

I thought how different they are from Mrs. Snelling, who goes about making trouble. Tomorrow Rene and I go on the trip up the Hudson, if it doesn't rain.

October 12

COLUMBUS DAY, a day to appreciate what the man did for us, having just taken a very safe boat ride up the Hudson River.

181

We left early yesterday. The streets were still wet from a nighttime rain when we left, but the sun shone gloriously as Charley drove us to the docks of New York in our barouche. I felt as if I was taking off for an exciting adventure with Rene.

When we reached the pier, I could smell the water before I saw it.

The docks are so exciting, I told Rene, and he told me that even though he comes here to his warehouse and office every day, he can't get over that feeling of excitement when he first sees the docks, and the ships lined up to go to faraway places. We rode right past the pier where his warehouse is, and on the side, in large yellow letters, is written, "Dumarest Bros. Silk Importing." Oh, I near lost my breath when I saw it.

Crowds were assembling either to board the ship or to watch it leave. Its name is the *Maid Marian*. It was flying all kinds of colorful flags, and there was music playing. Oh, I thrilled to the sight of it. And I thought how Daddy would like it, too.

We went up the gangplank to board and were shown immediately to our parlor suite, where we might have privacy if we wished it, yet where we had large enough windows to look out and see the scenery. Our attendant was most considerate, asking if we wanted any beverage. Tea, perhaps? Or a tray of coffee and buns? We said yes. I wanted to experience everything.

Our room was very well appointed, with rich woodworking and wallpaper and paintings of sailing ships on the walls. The curtains and bedspread matched, and the rug on the floor was rich, indeed. All the fittings in the bathroom were brass. I bounced on the bed, and then sat proper-like with Rene at a small table with silk-covered chairs to take our repast.

It wasn't long before the whistle sounded and I felt the boat move. I rushed to the window and saw the big side paddles turning around and around and splashing water. What a sight! They could hypnotize a person. I could watch them forever.

We went outside to the promenade deck to wave at the people on the dock. I saw Charley in the crowd and waved to him. Then we found deck chairs and Rene sent for a blanket for me, and we settled in to watch the scenery with everyone else.

And what scenery! It wasn't long before the docks and skyline of New York were behind us, and Rene was pointing out the small towns of New Jersey across the river. It looked like a patchwork quilt of houses and trees and docks and church spires and small boats on the water.

Soon after that, the towns disappeared and there was nothing but the greenery of woods and fields. And then we came upon the Palisades, which looked like great rocks reaching up into the blue sky.

We stayed in our deck chairs watching the scenery until lunchtime, then went into the dining room for a lovely repast. The best was the fresh vegetable soup. Oh, I wish I had that recipe. It had all kinds of vegetables and a very special taste and was perfect for lunch after coming in from outside.

After lunch we were able to see some very large houses along the cliffs of the Hudson. Rene said they were the homes of the rich Hudson River families, whose names went back to the Revolutionary War and before.

All in all, it was a lovely trip. We went all the way to Albany, where the boat docked and we got off. So did a lot of others, being that it is the state's capital. Rene hailed a carriage, and we were taken to a lovely restaurant, with sparkling chandeliers and soft music, for supper. It looked out on the water. Once again the food was delicious.

After supper we walked the town a bit and then went to our hotel, where we soon retired for the night, being rendered tired by the fresh air.

This morning it was very cold, and we boarded our paddle steamer again for the trip home.

On the way back, I got to thinking about everything I've been through since I came up from the South, and what a different person I am.

I watched Rene when he wasn't looking at me. He is so handsome and gentle with me. How could I ever have questioned marrying him? What a child I'd been. Yet something is happening here that isn't supposed to happen. I am falling in love with him. And I'd promised myself I would never do that, because he holds the mortgage on my parents' plantation. Anyway, I don't really know what love is, do I?

We arrived home late, and Charley was on the dock to greet us. I fell asleep in the barouche on the way home.

19

October 16

I LOVE THIS time of year the best of all. Outside, every tree on our road is standing like a soldier in a new, bright uniform. Mornings are crisp, the sun is warm during the day, and nights are cold enough for a blanket. At home, I know, Daddy will be worrying about frost on his cotton.

But when all should be happy in our house, we seem to be going through the onset of some bad times. I write of it not to honor it, but so someday my grandchildren will know what it took to make our marriage.

Rene's mother arrived, finally. She came unannounced to the front door and stood there, a large woman dressed all in black, wearing a hat with a plume and announcing herself with arms outspread: "Charlotte is here."

She speaks of herself in the third person. It is very annoying.

With her was an attractive young girl whom she calls Lizette, who carries her bundles and sees to her every need. After hellos were said, Charlotte eyed me up and down and asked Rene, "Is she one of us?"

The question could have meant anything. Rene did not reply. I notice there is a lot he does not reply to with his mother. Anyway, we welcomed her and she was shown to her room.

An extra cot was brought in for Lizette, who never left her mistress's side.

As a matter of fact, Lizette hovers over the table when we eat, which makes me very nervous. I can't imagine what it does to Mrs. Moore and Bridget and even Charley, who has always taken it upon himself to serve Rene personally.

I am surprised that Charlotte does not taste Rene's food first to make sure he isn't being poisoned. So there we are at the table. Three people with four servants. It is awkward, to say the least. And Lizette goes into the kitchen, too, to fetch Charlotte's plate of food and see that she gets the best cut of everything. I can see that it tears at Rene's nerves.

The first night was horrible. "You're too fat," she said to me.

"She's having a child, Mother," Rene told her.

"She's still too fat."

I felt like crying, but I didn't.

Did I mention that she brought a fluffy little dog with her? The dog follows her wherever she goes and has already chased my cat, Patches, all over the house. The nasty little thing sits on the furniture and eats scraps from Charlotte's hand at the table. Rene is trying to ignore all of this, I can see. But I can also see how annoyed he is with her.

I don't know what kind of a visit this is going to be.

October 23

TODAY I FOUND myself in tears. I got up early to go to the kitchen and talk to the servants about the day's meals, but Charlotte was already there. She told me to go back to bed. I told her I always get up at this hour. That I like to see Rene off to work.

"He doesn't need to be seen off to work," she said. "And if he does, Charlotte will see to him. Take advantage of it while she is here."

I told her I wanted to plan the meals with the servants.

"That is for Charlotte to do," she told me briskly. "She is practiced at this. Now, Mrs. Moore, I know Rene doesn't like broccoli, so we'll get him some nice fresh corn for supper."

Mrs. Moore gave me a look of pure misery, and I left the kitchen. The nerve! These were my duties, after all. What right does she have to take over in my own house?

I went upstairs and found Rene shaving. "What's wrong, sweetheart?" he asked.

"Your mother has taken over the house," I said.

He told me she wouldn't be here long. I told him it was still my house. "Then tell her," he urged. "Put her on notice right from the be-

ginning that *you* are the Mistress of Dorchester." He calls me that when he teases me.
The Mistress of Dorchester.

I told him I couldn't do that. I was hoping
he would. "This is a women's thing, darling,"
he said. "Try talking to her nicely, and if that
doesn't work, I'll have a word with her. I
promise. But you must stand up for yourself
and not always see yourself through my per-
mission."

But I haven't spoken up. And she's been
here a week now. And I feel displaced. Like I
don't belong here at all. Like a child again, I
feel. Adrift in my own home.

October 24

THERE IS SOME good news anyway. The
Needlework Guild has come up with the
money to send Mr. Cutler, the Confederate

soldier, south. Oh, I couldn't wait to tell him.
When I went to give him the news, he put his
arms around me and kissed me and said I
was like a daughter to him. I am so glad he is
happy.

October 25

MY JOYOUS MOOD of yesterday has passed.
Today is Thursday, and every Thursday I bake
in the kitchen. Mrs. Moore goes home early.
Bridget makes the supper while I bake. But
this Thursday, Charlotte would not allow it.

"In your condition?" she said. "Child, go
and rest. Go for a walk. You'll be plenty busy
when the baby comes."

She just put herself in the kitchen in my
place and said she would make some nice tarts
for dessert. Did we want French tarts?

Oh, I feel so helpless!

It isn't even that I like cooking or baking. It's just the idea that she is putting me out of my own place. And Rene won't talk to her. I feel so betrayed.

October 26

JUST WHEN I thought things couldn't get any worse, they did. I noticed this evening at supper that Lizette is flirting with Rene. She insists on serving him, as well as Charlotte, and beats Charley to the punch all the time. They glare at each other across our heads at the table. Not only does she serve Rene, she purrs to him about how he should eat the right greens and how good this or that is for him. It takes away my appetite, and I feel nauseous. She is so obvious about it.

Then, without so much as a by your leave, Charlotte breaks into French with Rene. I know my French, but hers is much more practiced. Rene answers her in English, to give him credit. He will not fall into that trap with her.

I feel as if I don't belong here anymore. I feel as if I want to leave. If I can't be mistress of my own home, what role do I have? What is the use of everything?

October 27

CHARLOTTE INSISTS I have a tea and introduce her to the women of the neighborhood. "I am, after all, your mother-in-law," she says. "At home this would have been done already."

Bridget is helping me plan a tea. We have sent out invitations this very day. One thing I have noticed is that Charlotte can be quite charming when she wants to be. I suppose I should have taken it upon myself to do this tea for her already.

October 30

WELL, WE HAD the tea this afternoon and most of the women came, all except Mrs. Snelling. I suppose our house wasn't big enough to fit both her and my mother-in-law into it, and I am just as glad she stayed away.

Charlotte was a big hit. She talked about her chateau, her town house, and Paris. Of course, to all Americans this is just like a fairy tale. Rene thanked me tonight for having the tea for her. "Perhaps this is just what you two needed to get along," he said. But I don't think so.

October 31

I AM MISERABLE. Charlotte insists on following her own plan of action in the house, and it does not include me. She is all over at once, ordering the servants about. Bridget has become sullen. Mrs. Moore doesn't speak any more than necessary, and Charley stays out in the stables as much as he can.

How can I run a house this way? What will happen when she leaves? Will they resent me because I didn't stand up for them? I must do something, even to show my objections to the way things are going. Rene is so busy he is scarce home, and as long as he gets his breakfast and his supper he doesn't care how the house is run. And I can't complain to him all the time. I don't want to be a nag.

November 1

IT IS GETTING cold at night. We need an extra blanket. Rene has had Charley make fires in the hearths in the dining room and the parlor. I am still working on the baby's layette.

November 2

MY THOUGHTS turn more and more to home. Rene had said we should make the trip by the end of the month, so I can spend the winter months in the South with my family, but I wish to go sooner. I mentioned it to Bridget this morning, because she is to go with me, as well as Rene.

But Bridget caught on right away. "You want to leave because of the old lady," she said.

"Yes."

"Don't let her drive you away. Stand up to her."

"How?"

She thought for a moment. Then she told me how. "Go to her in the kitchen. Take out of her hands whatever she is doing and say, 'Now, Charlotte, you are visiting and we want you to be treated as a visitor, as the grand lady you are. So you just let Bridget and Mrs.

Moore and me handle things in the kitchen and go into the parlor and put your feet up and finish that blanket you were knitting for the baby. And I'll bring you a cup of tea.'"

I stared at her. "Will it work?"

"I guarantee it will."

"I can't do it. I just can't."

"You must, Rose. It's the only way."

It was after supper and we were on the side porch. Rene was in his study. I don't know where Charlotte was. "Let me think about it," I said. "I need to go somewhere where I can think about it." And I got up and walked around the side of the house. Where could I go? And then I knew.

"Go inside and get my warm cloak, Bridget, and trolley fare."

"What are you going to do?"

"Just do it."

She did. I put the cloak on and walked to the front of the house and waited for the trolley to the sand dunes. All the while Bridget was on me. I couldn't go alone. Rene would worry. "Then let him worry," I said. Maybe he needs to worry a bit, and all the while it was coming on to me that this was why I was doing it.

I was, in a sense, running away to make Rene worry.

What I really wanted was to go home, but this would have to do for now.

Bridget waited with me until the trolley came, and then I looked at her. "I'll be back on the last trolley. Don't tell anyone."

"The master will have my head," she complained.

"Don't tell him," I ordered. "You work for me, not for him." And then I boarded the trolley.

20

November 2 (continued)

IT WAS PAST twilight when I boarded the trolley, the melancholy of an autumn evening. There were more shadows than remnants of sunlight, and in the west the sky was streaked with red and purple.

There was nobody on the trolley but me.

"Where to, missy?" the conductor asked.

"The end of the line."

"Kind of late for a pretty little missy like you to be going that far."

I felt a pang of fear. "I have friends there," I said.

We started off. As we bumped along, the houses grew more and more distant from each other, less grand, and more lonesome. Yet there was a beauty about the sand dunes and salt marshes and the wind that swept through the grasses. In some places I saw children playing, and as if that were a signal to the babe inside me, he quickened. And I thought: Will he grow up here, running and playing at 1600 Dorchester, or will he grow up on another beach down south? I already knew what name to put on what I was doing.

I was running away. As surely as if I'd packed a bag and taken a trolley to the steamer line at the docks.

I was running away like a child. And if

Rene wanted me back, if he truly loved me, he would come and fetch me home.

If he truly loved me. I felt an ache inside. A knowing that made me realize why I was doing this. It wasn't being mistress of the house so much as it was wanting Rene to stand up to his mother for me. I wanted proof of his love. Childish, yes, but it was all I wanted at the moment. Even while I was angry with him for allowing his mother to come into our house and turn it all topsy-turvy.

Because then I knew. I loved him. I had all along and I was growing, daily, in my love for him. And this wasn't supposed to happen. I married him because of my parents, so they wouldn't lose their plantation, so Rene wouldn't be able to bring himself to foreclose on the plantation if he had to.

And now I'd fallen in love with him. And I was darned if I was going to love him if he didn't love me.

I needed him to come to me, to prove that he loved me.

I had a brief moment of panic then, thinking: What if Bridget obeys me and doesn't tell him where I've gone? I could be on the sand dunes all night! And then I thought: What if he is angry and doesn't want to come?

I quelled these fears quickly and sat back to enjoy the scenery, and before I knew it we were at the end of the line, where the trolley turned around, where the sand dunes and marshes beckoned.

I got off with a cheerful nod to the driver, as if I knew what I was about. There were a few scattered cottages around, so it wasn't completely the end of the world. Then I stood and watched the trolley disappear from sight.

I was alone. Except for the wind and the gentle lapping of the waves and the cry of the seagulls. Several were picking their way along the beach, and I wished I had brought some bread for them. I could have been the last woman on the face of the earth.

I felt a well of loneliness inside me. Why did I have to be the one out here in the wilderness when I was indeed the Mistress of Dorchester? Was I the vanquished one?

If Rene didn't come, I decided, by the time of the last trolley, I'd go back home. He would have failed in this test of his love for me, and I would have to leave. I'd go home and pack a bag and leave for Mama and Daddy's place tomorrow. I'd take Bridget with me.

I felt better now that I had a plan in place. I found a place to sit on the dunes to watch the gulls. And then I had a thought: Suppose Rene was hard at work and didn't miss me? It led back to Bridget again. If I knew her, she'd tell him. She was afraid of him and, though she served me, ultimately worked for him. I knew that.

I made myself comfortable. The sand was warm from the sun, but soon it would be cold on this early November evening. I knew that. I wished I had the means to make a fire. Why hadn't I thought of it? But no. That might attract attention.

What time did the last trolley come? Nine o'clock. Suppose Rene missed it? No, don't think of that.

I lay down on the sand and I thought of home. Of Benjamin and Mama and Daddy, of Heppi and her husband.

It was all as if they had never existed. Oh, I wanted to go home. I felt tears gathering inside me.

What would Mama say about all of this? No matter how much help she had, she was always the mistress of her kitchen, of the house. Everybody knew it. Why couldn't I be like her? Because I had failed was why. I'd failed to keep my household and so I'd failed in my marriage.

I looked up at the sky, at the faint outline of moon, the hint of gathering of stars.

It was then that I fell asleep.

21

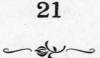

November 2 (continued)

I DON'T KNOW how long I slept, but it was one of those sleeps where you know you are sleeping yet can't wake up. I was so tired. I snuggled with my cloak around me. If I picked my head up, I knew the wind would be cold, but down here, close to the sand, there was no wind. There was no anything, except beautiful sleep.

The trolley roused me from sleep. The last trolley of the night, coming in the distance. Oh, how I dreaded its appearance. What if he wasn't on it?

I sat up as it got closer, seeing only its lights, like two ghost eyes coming at me. It came with a great shrug and a great heave, as if to say, "Sorry, Rose, I stayed away as long as I could."

The first man who got off was fat and roughly dressed and bore a lunch pail in hand. A workman. Then I held my breath and waited.

The second man was tall and slender with broad shoulders and a hat like my husband wore. He turned back to the driver of the trolley and spoke some words with him. I saw him hand up some money. Then he came onto the sand dunes and called my name.

I'd forgotten. If Rene had come to fetch me, he'd have to retain the trolley for the ride back. Why hadn't he had Charley hitch up the barouche? Because he didn't want to create a fuss is why. Rene liked to do things as quietly as possible.

Oh, my thoughts were reaching and clutching and falling. I couldn't get a grip on a decent idea.

And then he was close to me.

"Rose." The voice was not kindly. "Rose, I know you're here. Where are you?"

"Over here." I gathered up my things.

"What in the name of bloody hell are you doing out here in the dark? This isn't funny, Rose. You scared the devil out of me."

Never had I heard this tone before. He stood in front of me now. "What have you got to say to me, Rose?"

"I'm running away," I said.

For a moment or so he didn't answer. I was starting to be able to make his face out in the dark. "I wanted to go home," I said.

"You've picked the wrong direction."

"If you didn't come and find me I was going home tomorrow." I couldn't keep my voice from shaking.

He came toward me. He stood in front of me, silent for a moment. I could scarce see the expression on his face. "Rose, are you crazy? Has having a baby made you addled in the head? I didn't know where you were. Do you know what that does to a person?"

"I'm sorry. I had to leave. I didn't want to stay anymore."

"Does this all have to do with my mother?"

"Yes."

"You couldn't handle it like an adult? You had to run away like a child?"

"There is no handling her like an adult, Rene. You know that. Everybody is a child around her. All right for you and Adrian because you're grown. But I'm still a child inside. And I struggle every day to be grown-up and to please you."

He was silent. Then his arms came around me. "You do please me, Rose. You know that."

"Sometimes I don't," I said.

He told me then that I always did. "Didn't I marry you?" he asked.

"Why did you marry me, if you won't stand up for me with your mother?" I pushed.

He said he would, tonight when we got home. I told him it was too late, I didn't want it anymore. My mind was made up. Let her run the house. He grabbed me by the shoulders and said, "Rose, I wanted you to do it because I know you *can* do it. I don't want you treated like a child, by her or by me. I had confidence that you could do it, only you didn't. And I wanted you to see you could. I wanted you to have confidence in yourself."

"I'm too young for you," I said. "I'm only fifteen. Why did you marry me?"

"Because I love you. The question, I think, is why did you marry me?" he asked.

So I told him. "Because you hold the mortgage on our plantation. So you wouldn't foreclose on Mama and Daddy."

He said, "What?"

And I told him again why I married him.

He said, "What?" again. And then he said, "Where in God's name did you get that?"

"You do," I told him. Then he said he never heard such rot. I asked him, wasn't it true? And he said no, it isn't. But I was told, I said. And he asked by whom? So I told him, Amelia Caper.

"That girl was jealous of you," he told me. "She just wanted to ruin your happiness."

It all came to me then, like the surf behind me, sweeping everything clean. He didn't hold the mortgage. So it was all right to love him.

But then, I'd loved him all along, hadn't I? And tried not to?

"Come on," he said, "that driver won't wait forever, and you have to get home if you're going to pack and leave tomorrow."

"But I'm not leaving tomorrow," I told him. "I'm staying and going home with you at the end of the month as we planned."

So we got on the trolley and sat in back so we could talk. "I tried not to love you," I told him again. "I didn't want to love you."

"Well," he said, "you did a shabby job of it."

"I thought you held the mortgage," I went on, "and I married you to protect my parents. But I caught myself loving you all along and had to stop myself. What kind of person am I? Can you ever forgive me? What'll I do, Rene? What'll I do?"

"I'll work on the forgiving," he said. "We both will. We both have a lot of things to work on."

AUTHOR'S NOTE

WHILE BASED ON FACT, the story about Rose and Rene is fiction. They were my grandparents. Rose did live on a plantation and was fifteen when Rene, a silk merchant, came to visit. He did wed her and take her back to his house in Brooklyn. He did own two silk-importing houses with his brother. And he was a very wealthy man.

Rose had her first child at sixteen, and for that birth, and every other (she had five children), she went home to her mother and the plantation.

But in the early years of her marriage, she was still a child herself. I heard a story once about her having to be called in from skipping rope to feed the baby. I know she was a great influence on her neighborhood, but through her church, not through civic work. She died in 1961, much mourned, except by those closest to her. Her grandchildren did not know she existed. My mother (her first child) died shortly after I was born, and when my father remarried we were completely cut off from our mother's family.

I first saw Rose in her coffin. I was in the house on Dorchester Road only once, after she died. But I remember it well.

I don't know when Rene died. I only know that it was sometime between the two great wars and that on a visit to South America he was assassinated while going to collect a debt, and they sent his body home to his wife.

Up until recently these two people, who gave me a lot of my DNA, were quiet in my background. And then one day I thought, *I write stories about fifteen-year-old girls all the time, why not tell the one about my grand-mother and the first year of her marriage?*

So I set out to launch this story. When young people ask me what it is about, I am at a loss to say and usually end up saying, "It is my grandmother and grandfather, as I imagined them to be."

And then I add, "If you have grandparents, get to know them. Ask them questions. And if you don't, ask others about them. For we all have a Rene and a Rose in our lives. And someday you may need to know them."

BIBLIOGRAPHY

Beaufort, South Carolina, After the Civil War, 1865–1950. National Park Service, National Register of Historic Places, Beaufort Historic District, Beaufort, South Carolina.

Bridges, Anne Baker Leland, and Roy Williams III. *St. James Santee, Plantation Parish: History and Records, 1685–1925.* Spartanburg, S.C.: The Reprint Company Publishers, 1997.

PBS, American Experience. *America 1900.* http://www.pbs.org/wgbh/amex/1900.

Rosengarten, Theodore, with the journal of Thomas B. Chaplin (1822–1890). *Tombee: Portrait of a Cotton Planter.* New York: William Morrow & Co., 1986.

Snyder-Grenier, Ellen M., for the Brooklyn Historical Society. *Brooklyn! An Illustrated History*. Philadelphia: Temple University Press, 1996.

Sullivan, Mark. *Our Times, 1900–1925*. New York: Charles Scribner's Sons, 1939.

Younger, William Lee. *Old Brooklyn in Early Photographs, 1865–1929: 157 prints from the collection of the Long Island Historical Society*. New York: Dover Publications, 1978.

READER CHAT PAGE

1. How did the Civil War change Rose's island home? How did it affect Rose's family in particular?

2. Why does Rose think she must never let on that she knows about the mortgage? What do you think Amelia's real rationale was in telling Rose to keep it a secret?

3. How do Rose's and Rene's attitudes about servants and housework differ?

4. What are some of the incidents that confirm to Rose that she has chosen the right husband?

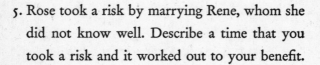

5. Rose took a risk by marrying Rene, whom she did not know well. Describe a time that you took a risk and it worked out to your benefit.

6. Rose adjusts to her new life in Brooklyn by becoming involved in the community, finding charitable causes and continuing the Southern tradition of Decoration Day. If you moved to a new place, what do you think you could do to make your own transition easier?

7. Rose was treated disrespectfully by Rene's mother, Charlotte, and their neighbor Mrs. Snelling. What do you think Rose learned from dealing with these unpleasant encounters?

8. How have attitudes about courtship and marriage changed since Rose's time?